Howard Heath

Sam Steele's Adventures on Land and Sea

Howard Heath

Sam Steele's Adventures on Land and Sea

ISBN/EAN: 9783337363215

Printed in Europe, USA, Canada, Australia, Japan

Cover: Foto ©Andreas Hilbeck / pixelio.de

More available books at **www.hansebooks.com**

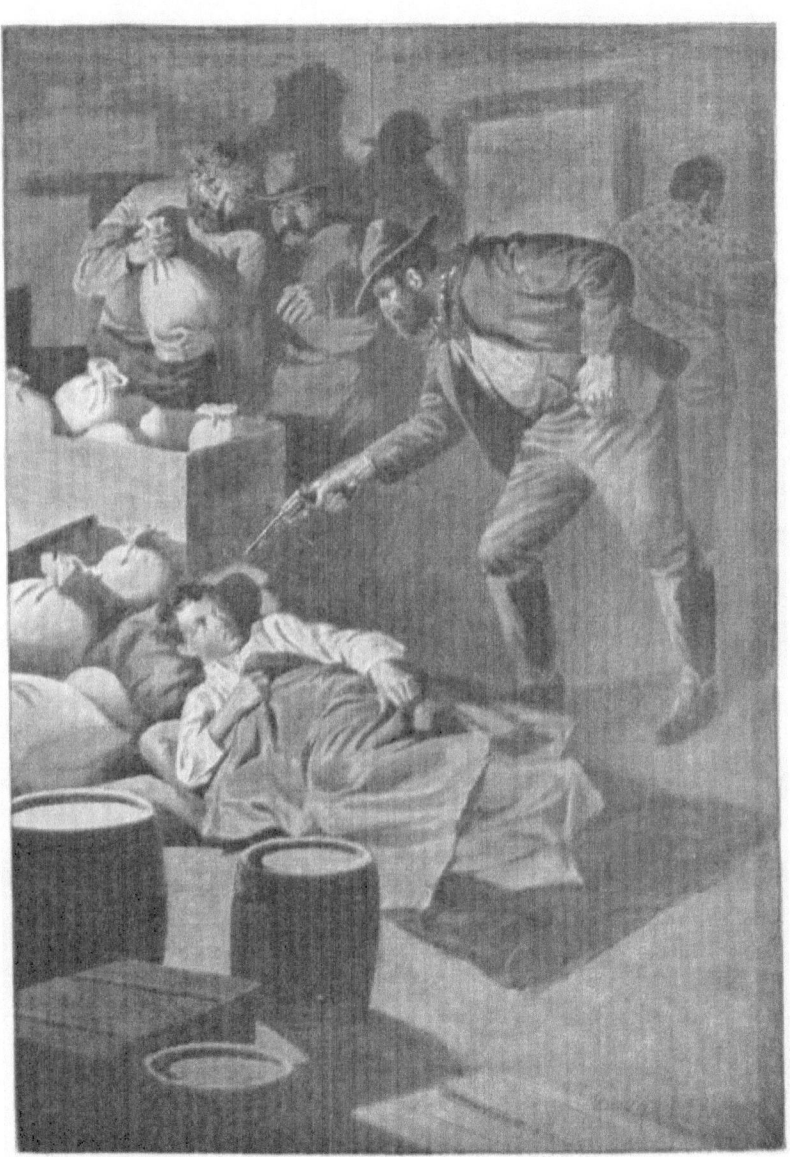

"Now, my lad, keep quiet an' you won't get hurt."

SAM STEELE'S

ADVENTURES
On Land
and Sea

By
CAPT. HUGH FITZGERALD

CHICAGO
THE REILLY & BRITTON CO.
PUBLISHERS

LIST OF CHAPTERS

CHAPTER

PAGE

I   I Hear Bad News 9

II   I Find a Relative 24

III   My Fortunes Improve 40

IV   I Ship Aboard the "Flipper" 54

V   "Nux" and "Bryonia" 66

VI   The Land of Mystery 83

VII   The Major 91

VIII   The Sands of Gold 110

IX   The Outlaws 124

X   The Rocking Stone 137

XI   The Cavern 153

XII   We Recover the Gold 169

XIII   The Catastrophe 184

XIV   Buried Alive! 193

XV   The Major Gives Chase 206

XVI   The Grave Captain Gay 219

XVII   We Give up the Ship 235

XVIII   Uncle Naboth's Revenge 247

XIX   The Conquest of Mrs. Ranck 257

XX   Steele, Perkins & Steele 270

LIST OF ILLUSTRATIONS
FROM ORIGINAL PAINTINGS BY
HOWARD HEATH

"Now, my lad, Keep Quiet an' You Won't get Hurt"
Frontispiece
Captured by the Gold-Hunters 97
A Hazardous Climb 177
"Leave the Room, Sir!" 231
"Here's the Treasure House, Sir!" 265

CHAPTER I.
I HEAR BAD NEWS.

"Sam—come here!"

It was Mrs. Ranck's voice, and sounded more bitter and stringent than usual.

I can easily recall the little room in which I sat, poring over my next day's lessons. It was in one end of the attic of our modest cottage, and the only room "done off" upstairs. The sloping side walls, that followed the lines of the roof, were bare except for the numerous pictures of yachts and other sailing craft with which I had plastered them from time to time. There was a bed at one side and a small deal table at the other, and over the little window was a shelf whereon I kept my meager collection of books.

"Sam! Are you coming, or not?"

With a sigh I laid down my book, opened the door, and descended the steep uncarpeted stairs to the lower room. This was Mrs. Ranck's living-room, where she cooked our meals, laid the table, and sat in her high-backed wooden rocker to darn and mend. It was a big, square room, which took up most of the space in the lower part of the house, leaving only a place for a small store-room at one end and the Captain's room at the other. At one side was the low, broad porch, with a door and two windows opening onto it, and at the other side, which was properly the back of the cottage, a small wing had been built which was occupied by

7

the housekeeper as her sleeping chamber.

As I entered the living-room in response to Mrs. Ranck's summons I was surprised to find a stranger there, seated stiffly upon the edge of one of the straight chairs and holding his hat in his lap, where he grasped it tightly with two big, red fists, as if afraid that it would get away. He wore an old flannel shirt, open at the neck, and a weather-beaten pea-jacket, and aside from these trade-marks of his profession it was easy enough to determine from his air and manner that he was a sea-faring man.

There was nothing remarkable about that, for every one in our little sea-coast village of Batteraft got a living from old ocean, in one way or another; but what startled me was to find Mrs. Ranck confronting the sailor with a white face and a look of mingled terror and anxiety in her small gray eyes.

"What is it, Aunt?" I asked, a sudden fear striking to my heart as I looked from one to the other in my perplexity.

The woman did not reply, at first, but continued to stare wildly at the bowed head of the sailor—bowed because he was embarrassed and ill at ease. But when he chanced to raise a rather appealing pair of eyes to her face she nodded, and said briefly:

"Tell him."

"Yes, marm," answered the man; but he shifted uneasily in his seat, and seemed disinclined to proceed further.

All this began to make me very nervous. Perhaps the

8

man was a messenger—a bearer of news. And if so his tale must have an evil complexion, to judge by his manner and Mrs. Ranck's stern face. I felt like shrinking back, like running away from some calamity that was about to overtake me. But I did not run. Boy though I was, and very inexperienced in the ways of life, with its troubles and tribulations, I knew that I must stay and hear all; and I braced myself for the ordeal.

"Tell me, please," I said, and my voice was so husky and low that I could scarce hear it myself. "Tell me; is —is it about—my father?"

The man nodded.

"It's about the Cap'n," he said, looking stolidly into Mrs. Ranck's cold features, as if striving to find in them some assistance. "I was one as sailed with him las' May aboard the 'Saracen.'"

"Then why are you here?" I cried, desperately, although even as I spoke there flashed across my mind a first realization of the horror the answer was bound to convey.

"'Cause the 'Saracen' foundered off Lucayas," said the sailor, with blunt deliberation, "an' went to the bottom, 'th all hands—all but me, that is. I caught a spar an' floated three days an' four nights, makin' at last Andros Isle, where a fisherman pulled me ashore more dead'n alive. That's nigh three months agone, sir. I've had fever sence—brain fever, they called it—so I couldn't bring the news afore."

I felt my body swaying slightly, and wondered if it

9

would fall. Then I caught at a ray of hope.

"But my father, Captain Steele? Perhaps he, also, floated ashore!" I gasped.

The sailor shook his head, regretfully.

"None but me was saved alive, sir," he answered, in a solemn voice. "The tide cast up a many o' the 'Saracen' corpses, while I lay in the fever; an' the fisher folks give 'em a decent burial. But they saved the trinkets as was found on the dead men, an' among 'em was Cap'n Steele's watch an' ring. I kep' 'em to bring to you. Here they be," he continued, simply, as he rose from his chair to place a small chamois bag reverently upon the table.

Mrs. Ranck pounced upon it and with trembling fingers untied the string. Then she drew forth my father's well-known round silver watch and the carbuncle ring he had worn upon his little finger ever since I could remember.

For a time no one spoke. I stared stupidly at the sailor, noticing that the buttons on his pea-jacket did not match and wondering if he always sewed them on himself. Mrs. Ranck had fallen back into her tall rocking-chair, where she gyrated nervously back and forth, the left rocker creaking as if it needed greasing. Why was it that I could not burst into a flood of tears, or wail, or shriek, or do anything to prove that I realized myself suddenly bereft of the only friend I had in all the world? There was an iron band around my forehead, and another around my chest. My brain was throbbing under one, and my heart trying desperately to beat under the other. Yet outwardly I must have appeared calm enough, and the fact filled me with shame and disgust.

An orphan, now, and alone in the world. This father whom the angry seas had engulfed was the only relative I had known since my sweet little mother wearied of the world and sought refuge in Heaven, years and years ago. And while father sailed away on his stout ship the "Saracen" I was left to the care of the hard working but crabbed and cross old woman whom I had come to call, through courtesy and convenience, "Aunt," although she was no relation whatever to me. Now I was alone in the world. Father, bluff and rugged, so strong and resourceful that I had seldom entertained a fear for his safety, was lying dead in the far away island of Andros, and his boy must hereafter learn to live without him.

The sailor, obviously uneasy at the effect of his ill tidings, now rose to go; but at his motion Mrs. Ranck seemed suddenly to recover the use of her tongue, and sternly bade him resume his seat. Then she plied him with questions concerning the storm and the catastrophe that followed it, and the man answered to the best of his ability.

Captain Steele was universally acknowledged one of the best and most successful seamen Batteraft had ever known. Through many years of trading in foreign parts he had not only become sole owner of the "Saracen," but had amassed a fortune which, it was freely stated in the town, was enough to satisfy the desires of any man. But this was merely guess-work on the part of his neighbors, for when ashore the old sailor confided his affairs to no one, unless it might have been to Mrs. Ranck. For the housekeeper was a different person when the Captain was ashore, recounting her own virtues so persistently, and seeming so solicitous for my comfort, that poor father stood somewhat in awe of her exceptional nobility of character. As soon as he had sailed she dropped the mask, and was often unkind; but I never minded this enough to worry him with complaints, so he was unconscious of her true nature.

Indeed, my dear father had been so seldom at home that I dreaded to cause him one moment's uneasiness. He was a reserved man, too, as is the case with so many sailors, and since the death of his dearly loved wife had passed but little of his time ashore. I am sure he loved me, for he always treated me with a rare tenderness; but he never would listen to my entreaties to sail with him.

"The sea's no place for a lad that has a comfortable home," he used to reply, in his slow, thoughtful way. "Keep to your studies, Sam, my boy, and you'll be a bigger man some day than any seaman of us all."

The Captain's brief visits home were the only bright spots in my existence, and because I had no one else to love I lavished upon my one parent all the affection of which I was capable. Therefore my present sudden bereavement was so colossal and far reaching in its effects upon my young life that it is no wonder the news staggered me and curiously dulled my senses.

Almost as if in a dream I heard Mrs. Ranck's fierce questions and the sailor's reluctant answers. And when he had told everything that he knew about the matter he got upon his feet and took my hands gently in both his big, calloused ones.

"I'm right sorry, lad, as ye've had this blow," he muttered, feelingly. "The Cap'n were a good man an' a kind master, an' many's a time I've heard him tell of his boy Sam. I s'pose he's left ye provided with plenty o' this world's goods, for he were a thrifty man and mostly in luck. But if ye ever run aground, lad, or find ye need a friend to cast a bowline, don't ye forget that Ned Britton'll stand by ye through thick an' thin!"

With this he wrung my hands until I winced under the pressure, and then he nodded briefly to Mrs. Ranck and hurried from the room.

The twilight had faded during the interview, and the housekeeper had lit a tallow candle. As Ned Britton's footsteps died away the woman bent forward to snuff the wick, and I noted a grim and determined look upon her features that was new to them. But her hands trembled somewhat, in spite of her assumed calmness, and the fact gave me a certain satisfaction. Her loss could not be compared with mine, but the Captain's death was sure to bring about a change in her fortunes, as well as my own.

She resumed her regular rocking back and forth, riveting her eyes the while upon my face. I did not sit, but leaned against the table, trying hard to think. And thus for a long time we regarded each other in silence.

Finally she cried out, sharply:

"Well, what are you a-goin' to do now?"

"In what way?" I asked, drearily.

"In every way. How are you goin' to live, fer one thing?"

"Why, much the same as I am doing now, I suppose," said I, trying to rouse myself to attend to what she was saying. "Father owned this house, which is now mine; and I'm sure there is considerable property besides, although the ship is lost."

"Fiddlesticks!" exclaimed Mrs. Ranck, scornfully.

I wondered what she meant by that, and looked my question.

"Your father didn't own a stick o' this house," she cried, in a tone that was almost a scream. "It's mine, an' the deed's in my own name!"

"I know," I replied, "but father has often explained that you merely held the deed in trust for me, until I became of age. He turned it over to you as a protection to me in case some accident should happen to him. Many times he has told me that this plan insured my having a home, no matter what happened."

"I guess you didn't understand him," she answered, an evil flash in her eye. "The facts is, this house were put into my name because the Cap'n owed me money."

"What for?" I asked.

"I've kep' ye in food an' clothes ever sence ye was a baby. Do ye s'pose that don't cost money?"

I stared at her bewildered.

"Didn't father furnish the money?"

"Not a cent. He jest let it run on, as he did any wages. An' it counts up big, that a-way."

14

"Then the house isn't mine, after all?"

"Not an inch of it. Not a stick ner a stone."

I tried to think what this would mean to me, and what reason the woman could have for claiming a right to my inheritance.

"Once," said I, musingly, "father told me how he had brought you here to save you from the poorhouse, or starvation. He was sorry for you, and gave you a home. That was while mother was living. Afterwards, he said, he trusted to your gratitude to take good care of me, and to stand my friend in place of my dead mother."

"Fiddlesticks" she snapped, again. It was the word she usually used to express contempt, and it sounded very disagreeable coming from her lips.

"The Cap'n must 'a' been a-dreamin' when he told you that stuff an' nonsense," she went on. "I've treated ye like my own son; there's no mistake about that. But I did it for wages, accordin' to agreement atween me an' the Cap'n. An' the wages wasn't never paid. When they got to be a big lump, he put the house in my name, to secure me. An' it's mine—ev'ry stick of it!"

My head was aching, and I had to press my hand to it to ease the pain. In the light of the one flickering candle Mrs. Ranck's hard face assumed the expression of a triumphant demon, and I drew back from it, shocked and repelled.

"If what you say is true," I said, listlessly, "I would rather you take the old home to wipe out the debt. Yet

15

father surely told me it was mine and it isn't like him to deceive me, or to owe any one money. However, take it, Aunt, if you like."

"I've got it," she answered; "an' I mean to keep it."

"I shall get along very well," said I, thinking, indeed, that nothing mattered much, now father was gone.

"How will you live?" she enquired.

"Why, there's plenty besides the house," I replied. "In father's room," and I nodded my head toward the door that was always kept locked in the Captain's absence, "there must be a great many valuable things stored. The very last time he was home he said that in case anything ever happened to him I would find a little fortune in his old sea-chest, alone."

"May be," rejoined the old woman, uneasily. "I hope *that* story o' his'n, at least, is true, for your sake, Sam. I hain't anything agin you; but right is right. An' the house don't cover all that's comin' to me, either. The Cap'n owed me four hundred dollars, besides the house, for your keep durin' all these years; an' that'll have to be paid afore you can honestly lay claim to a cent o' his property."

"Of course," I agreed, meekly enough, for all this talk of money wearied me. "But there should be much more than that in the chest, alone, according to what father said."

"Let's hope there is," said she. "You go to bed, now, for you're clean done up, an' no wonder. In the mornin' we'll both look into the Cap'n's room, an' see what's there. I ain't a-goin' to take no mean advantage o' you, Sam, you can depend on't. So go to bed. Sleep's the best cure-all fer troubles like yours."

This last was said in a more kindly tone, and I was glad to take her at her word and creep away to my little room in the attic.

CHAPTER II.
I FIND A RELATIVE.

It may have been hours that I sat at my little table, overcome by the bitterness of my loss. And for more hours I tossed restlessly upon my hard bed, striving in vain for comfort. But suddenly, as I recalled a little affectionate gesture of my father's, I burst into a flood of tears, and oh, what a relief it was to be able to cry — to sob away the load that had well-nigh overburdened my young heart!

After that last paroxysm of grief I fell asleep, worn out by my own emotions, and it was long past my usual hour for rising that I finally awoke.

In a moment, as I lay staring at the bright morning sunshine, the sorrow that had been forgotten in sleep swept over me like a flood, and I wept again at the thought of my utter loneliness and the dreadful fate that had overtaken my dear father. But presently, with the elasticity of youth, I was enabled to control myself, and turn my thoughts toward the future. Then I remembered that Mrs. Ranck and I were to enter the Captain's locked room, and take an inventory of his possessions, and I began hurriedly to dress myself, that this sad duty might be accomplished as soon as possible. The recollection of the woman's preposterous claims moved me to sullen anger. It seemed like a reflection on father's honesty to claim that he had been in her debt all these years, and I resolved that she should be paid every penny she demanded, that the

Captain's honor might remain untarnished in death, even as it had ever been during his lifetime.

As soon as I was ready I descended the stairs to the living room, where Mrs. Ranck sat rocking in her chair, just as I had left her the night before. She was always an early riser, and I noticed that she had eaten her own breakfast and left a piece of bacon and corn-bread for me upon the hearth.

She made no reply to my "good morning, Aunt," so I took the plate from the hearth and ate my breakfast in silence. I was not at all hungry; but I was young, and felt the need of food. Not until I had finished did Mrs. Ranck speak.

"We may as well look into the Cap'n's room, an' get it done with," she said. "It's only nat'ral as I should want to know if I'm goin' to get the money back I've spent on your keepin'."

"Very well," said I.

She went to a drawer of a tall bureau and drew out a small ivory box. Within this I knew were the keys belonging to my father. Never before had Mrs. Ranck dared to meddle with them, for the Captain had always forbidden her and everyone else to enter his room during his absence. Even now, when he was dead, it seemed like disobedience of his wishes for the woman to seize the keys and march over to the door of the sacred room. In a moment she had turned the lock and thrown open the door.

Shy and half startled at our presumption, I approached and peered over her shoulder.

Occasionally, indeed, I had had a glimpse of the interior of this little place, half chamber and half office; and, once or twice, when a little child, I had entered it to seek my father. Now, as I glanced within, it seemed to be in perfect order; but it struck me as more bare and unfurnished than I had ever seen it before. Father must have secretly removed many of the boxes that used to line the walls, for they were all gone except his big sea-chest.

The sight of the chest, however, reassured me, for it was in this that he had told me to look for my fortune, in case anything should happen to him.

The old woman at once walked over to the chest, and taking a smaller key from the ivory box, fitted it to the lock and threw back the lid with a bang.

"There's your fortune!" she said, with a sneer; "see if you can find it."

I bent over the chest, gazing eagerly into its depths. There was an old Bible in one end, and a broken compass in the other. But that was all.

Standing at one side, the woman looked into my astonished face and laughed mockingly.

"This was another o' the Cap'n's lies," she said. "He lied to you about ownin' the house; he lied to you about takin' me out o' charity; an' he lied to you about the fortune in this chest. An easy liar was Cap'n Steele, I must say!"

I shrank back, looking into her exultant eyes with horror in my own.

"How dare you say such things about my father?" I cried, in anger.

"How dare I?" she retorted; "why, because they're true, as you can see for yourself. Your father's deceived you, an' he's deceived me. I've paid out over four hundred dollars for your keep, thinkin' there was enough in this room to pay me back. An' now I stand to lose every penny of it, jest because I trusted to a lyin' sea-captain."

"You won't lose a dollar!" I cried, indignantly, while I struggled to keep back the tears of disappointment and shame that rushed to my eyes. "I'll pay you every cent of the money, if I live."

She looked at me curiously, with a half smile upon her thin lips.

"How?" she asked.

"I'll work and earn it."

"Pish! what can a boy like you earn? An' what's goin' to happen while you're earnin' it? One thing's certain, Sam Steele; you can't stay here an' live off'n a poor lone woman that's lost four hundred dollars by you already. You'll have to find another place."

"I'll do that," I said, promptly.

"You can have three days to git out," she continued, pushing me out of the room and relocking the door, although there was little reason for that. "And you can take whatever clothes you've got along with you. Nobody can say that Jane Ranck ain't acted like a Christian to ye, even if she's beat an' defrauded out'n

21

her just rights. But if ye should happen to earn any money, Sam, I hope you'll remember what ye owe me."

"I will," said I, coldly; and I meant it.

To my surprise Mrs. Ranck gave a strange chuckle, which was doubtless meant for a laugh—the first I had ever known her to indulge in. It fired my indignation to such a point that I cried out: "Shame!" and seizing my cap I rushed from the house.

The cottage was built upon a small hill facing the bay, and was fully a quarter of a mile distant from the edge of the village of Batteraft. From our gate the path led down hill through a little group of trees and then split in twain, one branch running down to the beach, where the shipping lay, and the other crossing the meadows to the village. Among the trees my father had built a board bench, overlooking the bay, and here I have known him to sit for hours, enjoying the beauty of the view, while the leafy trees overhead shaded him from the hot sun.

It was toward this bench, a favorite resort of mine because my father loved it, that I directed my steps on leaving Mrs. Ranck. At the moment I was dazed by the amazing discovery of my impoverished condition, and this, following so suddenly upon the loss of my father, nearly overwhelmed me with despair. But I knew that prompt action on my part was necessary, for the woman had only given me three days grace, and my pride would not suffer me to remain that long in a home where my presence was declared a burden. So I would sit beneath the trees and try to decide where to go and what to do.

But as I approached the place I found, to my astonishment, that a man was already seated upon the bench. He was doubtless a stranger in Batteraft, for I had never seen him before, so that I moderated my pace and approached him slowly, thinking he might discover he was on private grounds and take his leave.

He paid no attention to me, being engaged in whittling a stick with a big jack-knife. In appearance he was short, thick-set, and of middle age. His round face was lined in every direction by deep wrinkles, and the scant hair that showed upon his temples was thin and grey. He wore a blue flannel shirt, with a black kerchief knotted at the throat; but, aside from this, his dress was that of an ordinary civilian; so that at first I was unable to decide whether he was a sailor or a landsman.

The chief attraction in the stranger was the expression of his face, which was remarkably humorous. Although I was close by him, now, he paid no attention to my presence, but as he whittled away industriously he gave vent to several half audible chuckles that seemed to indicate that his thoughts were very amusing.

I was about to pass him and go down to the beach, where I might find a solitary spot for my musings, when the man turned his eyes up to mine and gave a wink that seemed both mysterious and confidential.

"It's Sam, ain't it?" he asked, with another silent chuckle.

"Yes, sir," I replied, resenting his familiarity while I wondered how he should know me.

"Cap'n Steele's son, I'm guessin'?" he continued.

"The same, sir," and I made a movement to pass on.

"Sit down, Sam; there's no hurry," and he pointed to the bench beside him.

I obeyed, wondering what he could want with me. Half turning toward me, he gave another of those curious winks and then suddenly turned grave and resumed his whittling.

"May I ask who you are, sir?" I enquired.

"No harm in that," he replied, with a smile that lighted his wrinkled face most comically. "No harm in the world. I'm Naboth Perkins."

"Oh," said I, without much interest.

"Never heard that name before, I take it?"

"No, sir."

"Do you remember your mother?"

"Not very well, sir," I answered, wondering more and more. "I was little more than a baby when she died, you know."

"I know," and he nodded, and gave an odd sort of grunt. "Did you ever hear what her name was, afore she married the Cap'n?"

"Oh, yes!" I cried, suddenly enlightened. "It was Mary Perkins."

Then, my heart fluttering wildly, I turned an intent

and appealing gaze upon the little man beside me.

Naboth Perkins was seized with another of those queer fits of silent merriment, and his shoulders bobbed up and down until a cough caught him, and for a time I feared he would choke to death before he could control the convulsions. But at last he recovered and wiped the tears from his eyes with a brilliant red handkerchief.

"I'm your uncle, lad," he said, as soon as he could speak.

This was news, indeed, but news that puzzled me exceedingly.

"Why have I never heard of you before?" I asked, soberly.

"Haven't ye?" he returned, with evident surprise.

"Never."

He looked the stick over carefully, and cut another notch in it.

"Well, for one thing," he remarked, "I've never been in these parts afore sence the day I was born. Fer another thing, it stands to reason you was too young to remember, even if Mary had talked to ye about her only brother afore she died an' quit this 'ere sublunatic spear. An', fer a third an' last reason, Cap'n Steele were a man that had little to say about most things, so it's fair to s'pose he had less to say about his relations. Eh?"

"Perhaps it is as you say, sir."

"Quite likely. Yet it's mighty funny the Cap'n never let drop a word about me, good or bad."

"Were you my father's friend?" I asked, anxiously.

"That's as may be," said Mr. Perkins, evasively. "Friends is all kinds, from acquaintances to lovers. But the Cap'n an me wasn't enemies, by a long shot, an' I've been his partner these ten year back."

"His partner!" I echoed, astonished.

The little man nodded.

"His partner," he repeated, with much complacency. "But our dealin's together was all on a strict business basis. We didn't hobnob, ner gossip, ner slap each other on the back. So as fer saying we was exactly friends—w'y, I can't honestly do it, Sam."

"I understand," said I, accepting his explanation in good faith.

"I came here at this time," continued Mr. Perkins, addressing his speech to the jack-knife, which he held upon the palm of his hand, "to see Cap'n Steele on an important business matter. He had agreed to meet me. But I saw Ned Britton at the tavern, las' night, an' heerd fer the first time that the 'Saracen' had gone to Davy Jones an' took the Cap'n with her. So I come up here to have a little talk with you, which is his son and my own nevvy."

"Why didn't you come up to the house?" I enquired.

Mr. Perkins turned upon me his peculiar wink, and his shoulders began to shake again, till I feared more convulsions. But he suddenly stopped short, and with abrupt gravity nodded his head at me several times.

"The woman!" he said, in a low voice. "I jest can't abide women. 'Specially when they's old an' given to argument, as Ned Britton says this one is."

I sympathized with him, and said so. Whereat my uncle gave me a look gentle and kindly, and said in a friendly tone:

"Sam, my boy, I want to tell you all about myself, that's your blood uncle an' no mistake; but first I want you to tell me all about yourself. You're an orphan, now, an' my dead sister's child, an' I take it I'm the only real friend you've got in the world. So now, fire away!"

There was something about the personality of Naboth Perkins that invited confidence; or perhaps it was my loneliness and need of a friend that led me to accept this astonishing uncle in good faith. Anyway, I did not hesitate to tell him my whole story, including my recent grief at the news of my dear father's death and the startling discovery I had just made that I was penniless and in debt for my living to Mrs. Ranck.

"Father has often told me," I concluded, "that the house was mine, and had been put in Mrs. Ranck's name because he felt she was honest, and would guard my interests in his absence. And he told me there was a store of valuable articles in his room, which he had been accumulating for years, and that the old sea-chest alone contained enough to make me independent. But when we examined the room this morning everything was gone, and the chest was empty. I don't know what

27

to think about it, I'm sure; for father never lied, in spite of what Mrs. Ranck says."

Uncle Naboth whistled a sailor's hornpipe in a slow, jerky, and altogether dismal fashion. When it was quite finished, even to the last quavering bar, he said:

"Sam, who kept the keys to the room, an' the chest?"

"Mrs. Ranck."

"M—m. Was the room dark, an' all covered over with dust, when you went in there this mornin'?"

"I——I don't think it was," I answered, trying to recollect. "No! I remember, now. The blind was wide open, and the room looked clean and in good order."

"Sailors," remarked Mr. Perkins, impressively, "never is known to keep their rooms in good order. The Cap'n been gone five months an' more. If all was straight the dust would be thick on everything."

"To be sure," said I, very gravely.

"Then, Sam, it stands to reason the ol' woman went inter the room while you was asleep, an' took out everything she could lay her hands on. Cap'n Steele didn't lie to you, my boy. But he made the mistake of thinkin' the woman honest. She took advantage of the fact that the Cap'n was dead, an' couldn't prove nothin'. And so she robbed you."

The suspicion had crossed my mind before, and I was not greatly surprised to hear my uncle voice it.

"Then, can't we make her give it up?" I asked. "If she

has done such a wicked thing, it seems as though we ought to accuse her of it, and make her give me all that belongs to me."

Uncle Naboth rose slowly from the bench, settled his felt hat firmly upon his head, pulled down his checkered vest, and assumed a most determined bearing.

"You wait here," he said, "an' I'll beard the she-tiger in her den, an' see what can be done."

Then he gave a great sigh, and turning square around, marched stiffly up the path that led to the house.

CHAPTER III.
MY FORTUNES IMPROVE.

I awaited with as much patience as I could muster the result of the venture. I was proud of Uncle Naboth's bravery, and hoped he would be successful. Surely the brief interview with my newly acquired relative had caused a great change in my future prospects, for it was not likely that my mother's brother would desert me in my extremity. I had left the house that was now no longer my home without a single friend to whom I could turn, and behold, here was a champion waiting to espouse my cause! Mr. Perkins was somewhat peculiar in his actions, it is true, but he was my uncle and my dead father's partner, and already I was beginning to have faith in him.

It was a full half hour before I saw him coming back along the path; but now he no longer strutted with proud determination. Instead, his whole stout little body drooped despondently; his hat was thrust back from his forehead, and upon his deeply wrinkled face stood big drops of perspiration.

"Sam," said he, standing before me with a rather sheepish air, "I were wrong, an' I beg your pardon. That woman ain't no she-tiger. I mis-stated the case. She's a she-devil!"

The words were laden with disgust and indignation. Uncle Naboth drew out his gorgeous handkerchief and wiped his face with it. Then he dropped upon the bench and pushed his big hands deep into his capacious pockets, with the air of a man crushed and defeated.

I sighed.

"Then she refused to give up the property?"

"Give up? She'd die first. Why, Sam, the critter tried to brain me with a gridiron! Almost, my boy, you was an orphan agin. He who fights an' runs away may n't get much credit for it, but he's a durned sight safer ner a dead man. The Perkinses was allus a reckless crew; but sooner 'n face that female agin I'd tackle a mad bull!"

"Won't the law help us?" I asked.

"The law!" cried Mr. Perkins, in a voice of intense horror. "W'y, Sam, the law's more to be dreaded than a woman. It's an invention of the devil to keep poor mortals from becomin' too happy in this 'ere vale o' tears. My boy, if ye ever has to choose between the law an' a woman, my advice is to commit suicide at once. It's quicker an' less painful."

"But the law stands for justice," I protested.

"That's the bluff it puts up," said Uncle Naboth, "but it ain't so. An' where's your proof agin Mrs. Ranck, anyhow? Cap'n Steele foolishly put the house in her name. If she ain't honest enough to give it up, no one can take it from her. An' he kep' secret about the fortune that was left in his room, so we can't describe the things you've been robbed of. Altogether, it's jest a hopeless case. The she-devil has made up her mind to inherit your fortune, an' you can't help

31

yourself."

As I stared into the little man's face the tears came into my eyes and blurred my sight. He thrust the red handkerchief into my hand, and I quickly wiped away the traces of unmanly weakness. And when I could see plainly again my uncle was deeply involved in one of his fits of silent merriment, and his shoulders were shaking spasmodically. I waited for him to cough and choke, which he proceeded to do before regaining his gravity. The attack seemed to have done him good, for he smiled at my disturbed expression and laid a kindly hand on my shoulder.

"Run up to the house, my lad, an' get your bundle of clothes," he said. "I'll be here when you get back. Don't worry over what's gone. I'll take care o' you, hereafter."

I gave him a grateful glance and clasped his big, horny hands in both my own.

"Thank you, uncle," said I; "I don't know what would have become of me if you had not turned up just as you did."

"Lucky; wasn't it, Sam? But run along and get your traps."

I obeyed, walking slowly and thoughtfully back to the house. When I tried to raise the latch I found the door locked.

"Mrs. Ranck!" I called. "Mrs. Ranck, let me in, please. I've come for my clothes."

There was no answer. I rattled the latch, but all in

vain. So I sat down upon the steps of the porch, wondering what I should do. It was a strange and unpleasant sensation, to find myself suddenly barred from the home in which I had been born and wherein I had lived all my boyhood days. It was only my indignation against this selfish and hard old woman that prevented me from bursting into another flood of tears, for my nerves were all unstrung by the events of the past few hours. However, anger held all other passion in check for the moment, and I was about to force an entrance through the side window, as I had done on several occasions before, when the sash of the window in my own attic room was pushed up and a bundle was projected from it with such good aim that it would have struck my head, had I not instinctively dodged it.

Mrs. Ranck's head followed the bundle far enough to cast a cruel and triumphant glance into my upturned face.

"There's your duds. Take 'em an' go, you ongrateful wretch!" she yelled. "An' don't ye let me see your face again until you come to pay me the money you owes for your keepin'."

"Please, Mrs. Ranck," I asked, meekly, "can I have my father's watch and ring?"

"No, no, no!" she screamed, in a fury. "Do ye want to rob me of everything? Ain't you satisfied to owe me four hundred dollars a'ready?"

"I——I'd like some keepsake of father's," I persisted, well knowing this would be my last chance to procure it. "You may keep the watch, if you'll give me the

33

ring."

"I'll keep'm both," she retorted. "You'll get nothin' more out'n me, now or never!"

Then she slammed down the window, and refused to answer by a word my further pleadings. So finally I picked up the bundle and, feeling miserable and sick at heart, followed the path back to the little grove.

"It didn't take you very long, but that's all the better," said my uncle, shutting his clasp-knife with a click and then standing up to brush the chips from his lap. "We two'll go to the tavern, an' talk over our future plans."

Silently I walked by the side of Naboth Perkins until we came to the village. I knew everyone in the little town, and several of the fishermen and sailors met me with words of honest sympathy for my loss. Captain Steele had been the big man of Batteraft, beloved by all who knew him despite his reserved nature, and these simple villagers, rude and uneducated but kindly hearted, felt that in his death they had lost a good friend and a neighbor of whom they had always been proud. Not one of them would have refused assistance to Captain Steele's only son; but they were all very poor, and it was lucky for me that Uncle Naboth had arrived so opportunely to befriend me.

Having ordered a substantial dinner of the landlord of "The Rudder," Mr. Perkins gravely invited me to his private room for a conference, and I climbed the rickety stairs in his wake.

The chamber was very luxurious in my eyes, with

its rag carpet and high-posted bed, its wash-stand and rocking-chair. I could not easily withhold my deference to the man who was able to hire it, and removing my cap I sat upon the edge of the bed while Uncle Naboth took possession of the rocking-chair and lighted a big briar pipe.

Having settled himself comfortably by putting his feet upon the sill of the open window, he remarked:

"Now, Sam, my lad, we'll talk it all over."

"Very well, sir," I replied, much impressed.

"In the first place, I'm your father's partner, as I said afore. Some years ago the Cap'n found he had more money'n he could use in his own business, an' I'd saved up a bit myself, to match it. So we put both together an' bought a schooner called the 'Flipper', w'ich I'm free to say is the best boat, fer its size an' kind, that ever sailed the Pacific."

"The Pacific!"

"Naterally. Cap'n Steele on the Atlantic, an' Cap'n Perkins on the Pacific. In that way we divided up the world between us." He stopped to wink, here, and began his silent chuckle; but fortunately he remembered the importance of the occasion and refrained from carrying it to the choking stage. "I s'pose your father never said naught to you about this deal o' ours, any more'n he did to that she-bandit up at the house. An' it's lucky he didn't, or the critter'd be claimin' the 'Flipper', too, an' then you an' I'd be out of a job!"

He winked again; solemnly, this time; and I sat still

and stared at him.

"Howsomever, the 'Flipper' is still in statute loo, an' thank heaven fer that! I made sev'ral voyages in her to Australy, that turned out fairly profitably, an' brought the Cap'n an' me some good bits o' money. So last year we thought we'd tackle the Japan trade, that seemed to be lookin' up. It looked down agin as soon as I struck the pesky shores, an' a month ago I returned to 'Frisco a sadder an' a wiser man. Not that the losses was so great, Sam, you understand; but the earnin's wasn't enough to buy a shoe-string.

"So I sailed cross-lots to Batteraft to consult with my partner, which is Cap'n Steele, as to our next voyage, an' the rest o' the story you know as well as I do. Your father bein' out o' the firm, from no fault o' his'n, his son is his nateral successor. So I take it that hereafter we'll have to consult together."

My amazed expression amused him exceedingly, but I found it impossible just then to utter a single word. Uncle Naboth did not seem to expect me to speak, for after lighting his pipe again he continued, with an air of great complacency:

"It mought be said that, as you're a minor, I stands as your rightful guardeen, an' have a right to act for you 'til you come of age. On the other hand, you mought claim that, bein' a partner, your size an' age don't count, an' you've a right to be heard. Howsomever, we won't go to law about it, Sam. The law's onreliable. Sometimes it's right, an' mostly it's wrong; but it ain't never to be trusted by an honest man. If you insist on dictatin' what this partnership's goin' to do, you'll probably run it on a rock in two

36

jerks of a lamb's tail, for you haven't got the experience old Cap'n Steele had; but if you're satisfied to let me take the tiller, an' steer you into harbor, why, I'll accept the job an' do the best I can at it."

"Uncle Naboth," I replied, earnestly, "had you not been an honest man I would never have known you were my father's partner, or that he had any interest in your business. But you've been more than honest. You've been kind to me; and I am only too glad to trust you in every way."

"Well spoke, lad!" cried Mr. Perkins, slapping his knee delightedly. "It's what I had a right to expect in poor Mary's boy. We're sure to get along, Sam, and even if I don't make you rich, you'll never need a stout friend while your Uncle Nabe is alive an' kickin'!"

Then we both stood up, and shook hands with great solemnity, to seal the bargain. After which my friend and protector returned to his rocker and once more stretched his feet across the window sill.

"How much property belongs to me, Uncle?" I asked.

"We never drew up any papers. Cap'n Steele knew as he could trust me, an' so papers wa'n't necessary. He owned one-third interest in the 'Flipper', an' supplied one half the money to carry on the trade. That made it mighty hard to figure out the profits, so we gen'ly lumped it, to save brain-work. Of course your father's been paid all his earnin's after each voyage was over, so accounts is settled up to the Japan trip. Probably the money I gave him was in the sea-chest, an' that old she-pirate up to the house grabbed it with the other

37

things. The Japan voyage was a failure, as I told you; but there's about a thousand dollars still comin' to the Cap'n—which means it's comin' to you, Sam—an' the ship's worth a good ten thousand besides."

I tried to think what that meant to me.

"It isn't a very big sum of money, is it, Uncle?" I asked, diffidently.

"That depends on how you look at it," he answered. "Big oaks from little acorns grow, you know. If you leave the matter to me, I'll try to make that thousand sprout considerable, before you come of age."

"Of course I'll leave it to you," said I. "And I am very grateful for your kindness, sir."

"Don't you turn your gratitude loose too soon, Sam. I may land your fortunes high an' dry on the rocks, afore I've got through with 'em. But if I do it won't be on purpose, an' we'll sink or swim together. An' now, that bein' as good as settled, the next thing to argy is what you're a-goin' to do while I'm sailin' the seas an' makin' money for you."

"What would you suggest?" I asked.

"Well, some folks might think you ought to have more schoolin'. How old are you?"

"Sixteen, sir."

"Can you read an' write, an' do figgers?"

"Oh, yes; I've finished the public school course," I replied, smiling at the simple question.

"Then I guess you've had study enough, my lad, and are ready to go to work. I never had much schoolin' myself, but I've managed to hold my own in the world, in spite of the way letters an' figgers mix up when I look at 'em. Not but what eddication is a good thing; but all eddication don't lay in schools. Rubbin' against the world is what polishes up a man, an' the feller that keeps his eyes open can learn somethin' new every day. To be open with you, Sam, I need you pretty bad on the 'Flipper', to keep the books an' look after the accounts, an' do writin' an' spellin' when letters has to be writ. On the last trip I put in four days hard work, writin' a letter that was only three lines long. An' I'm blamed if the landsman I sent it to didn't telegraph me for a translation. So, if you're willin' to ship with the firm of Perkins & Steele, I'll make you purser an' chief clerk."

"I should like that!" I answered, eagerly.

"Then the second p'int's settled. There's only one more. The 'Flipper' is lyin' in the harbor at 'Frisco. When shall we join her, lad?"

"I'm ready now, sir."

"Good. I've ordered a wagon to carry us over to the railroad station at four o'clock, so ye see I had a pretty good idea beforehand what sort o' stuff Mary's boy was made of. Now let's go to dinner."

CHAPTER IV.
I SHIP ABOARD THE "FLIPPER."

When the two-seated spring wagon drew up before the tavern door quite a crowd of idle villagers assembled to see us off, and among them I noticed my father's old sailor, Ned Britton. Uncle Naboth climbed aboard at once, but I stayed to shake the hands held out to me and to thank the Batteraft people for their hearty wishes for my future prosperity. I think they were sorry to see me go, and I know I felt a sudden pang of regret at parting from the place where I had lived so long and the simple villagers who had been my friends.

When at last I mounted to the rear seat of the wagon and sat beside my uncle, I was astonished to find Ned Britton established beside the driver.

"Are you going with us?" I asked.

The sailor nodded.

"It's like this," remarked Mr. Perkins, as we rolled away from the tavern, "this man belonged to my old partner, Cap'n Steele, an' stuck to his ship 'til she went down. Also he's put himself out to come here an' tell us the news, and it ain't every sailor as'll take the trouble to do such a job. Therefore, Ned Britton bein' at present without a ship, I've asked him to take a berth aboard the 'Flipper.'"

"That was kind of you, Uncle," I said, pleased at this

evidence of my relative's kindly nature.

"An honest sailor ain't to be sneezed at," continued Uncle Naboth, with one of his quaint winks. "If Ned Britton were faithful to the 'Saracen' he'll be faithful to the 'Flipper.' An' that's the sort o' man we want."

Britton doubtless overheard every word of this eulogy, but he gazed stolidly ahead and paid no attention to my uncle's words of praise.

We reached the railway station in ample time for the train, and soon were whirling away on our long journey into the golden West.

No incident worthy of note occurred on our way across the continent, although I might record a bit of diplomacy on the part of Uncle Naboth that illustrates the peculiar shrewdness I have always found coupled with his native simplicity.

Just before our train drew into Chicago, where we were to change cars and spend the best part of a day, my uncle slipped into my hand a long, fat pocket-book, saying:

"Hide that in your pocket, Sam, and button it up tight."

"What's your idea, Uncle Nabe?" I asked.

"Why, we're comin' to the wickedest city in all the world, accordin' to the preachers; an' if it ain't that, it's bad enough, in all conscience. There's robbers an' hold-up men by the thousands, an' if one of 'em got hold of me I'd be busted in half a second. But none of 'em would think of holdin' up a boy like you; so the money's safe in your pocket, if you don't go an' lose it."

"I'll try not to do that, sir," I returned; but all during the day the possession of the big pocket-book made me nervous and uneasy. I constantly felt of my breast to see that the money was still safe, and it is a wonder my actions did not betray to some sly thief the fact that I was concealing the combined wealth of our little party.

No attempt was made to rob us, however, either at Chicago or during the remainder of the journey to the Pacific coast, and we arrived at our destination safely and in good spirits.

Uncle Naboth seemed especially pleased to reach San Francisco again.

"This car travellin'," he said, "is good enough for landsmen that don't know of anything better; but I'd rather spend a month at sea than a night in one of them stuffy, dangerous cars, that are likely to run off'n the track any minute."

Ned Britton and I accompanied Mr. Perkins to a modest but respectable lodging-house near the bay, where we secured rooms and partook of a hearty breakfast. Then we took a long walk, and I got my first sight of the famous "Golden Gate." I was surprised at the great quantity of shipping in the bay, and as I looked over the hundreds of craft at anchor I wondered curiously which was the "Flipper," of which I was part owner—the gallant ship whose praises Uncle Naboth had sung so persistently ever since we left Batteraft.

After luncheon we hired a small boat, and Ned Britton undertook to row us aboard the "Flipper," which had been hidden from our view by a point of land. I own that after my uncle's glowing descriptions of her I expected to see a most beautiful schooner, with lines even nobler than those of the grand old "Saracen," which had been my father's pride for so many years. So my disappointment may be imagined when we drew up to a grimy looking vessel of some six hundred tons, with discolored sails, weather-worn rigging and a glaring need of fresh paint.

Ned Britton, however, rested on his oars, studied the ship carefully, and then slowly nodded his head in approval.

"Well, what d'ye think o' her?" asked Uncle Naboth, relapsing into one of his silent chuckles at the expression of my face.

"She looks rather dirty, sir," I answered, honestly.

"The 'Flipper' ain't quite as fresh as a lily in bloom, that's a fact," returned my uncle, in no ways discomfited by my remark. "She wasn't no deebutantee when I bought her, an' her clothes has got old, and darned and patched, bein' as we haven't been near to a Paris dressmaker. But I've sailed in her these ten years past, Sam, an' we're both as sound as a dollar."

"She ought to be fast, sir," remarked Britton, critically.

Mr. Perkins laughed—not aloud, but in his silent, distinctly humorous way.

"She *is* fast, my lad, w'ich is a virtue in a ship if it

43

ain't in a woman. And in some other ways, besides, the 'Flipper' ain't to be sneezed at. As for her age, she's too shy to tell it, but I guess it entitles her to full respect."

We now drew alongside, and climbed upon the deck, where my uncle was greeted by a tall, lank man who appeared to my curious eyes to be a good example of a living skeleton. His clothes covered his bones like bags, and so thin and drawn was his face that his expression was one of constant pain.

"Morn'n', Cap'n," said Uncle Naboth, although it was afternoon.

"Morn'n', Mr. Perkins," returned the other, in a sad voice. "Glad to see you back."

"Here's my nevvy, Sam Steele, whose father were part owner but got lost in a storm awhile ago."

"Glad to see you, sir," said the Captain, giving my hand a melancholy shake.

"An' here's Ned Britton, who once sailed with Cap'n Steele," continued my uncle. "He'll sign with us, Cap'n Gay, and I guess you'll find him A No. 1."

"Glad to see you, Britton," repeated the Captain, in his dismal voice. If the lanky Captain was as glad to see us all as his words indicated, his expression fully contradicted the fact.

Britton saluted and walked aft, where I noticed several sailors squatting upon the deck in careless attitudes. To my glance these seemed as solemn and joyless as their Captain; but I acknowledge that on this first visit everything about the ship was a disappointment to me, perhaps because I had had little experience with trading vessels and my mind was stored with recollections of the trim "Saracen."

Below, however, was a comfortable cabin, well fitted up, and Uncle Naboth showed me a berth next to his own private room which was to be my future home. The place was little more than a closet, but I decided it would do very well.

"I thought *you* were the captain of the 'Flipper,' Uncle Naboth," said I, when we were alone.

"No; I'm jest super-cargo," he replied, with his usual wink. "You see, I wasn't eddicated as a sailor, Sam, an' never cared to learn the trade. Cap'n Gay is one o' the best seamen that ever laid a course, so I hire him to take the ship wherever I want to go. As fer the cargo, that's my 'special look-out, an' it keeps me busy enough, I can tell you. I'm a nat'ral born trader, and except fer that blamed Japan trip, I ain't much ashamed of my record."

"Will you go to Australia again?" I asked.

"Not jest now, Sam. My next venture's goin' to be a bit irregular—what you might call speculative, an' extry-hazardous. But we'll talk that over tonight, after supper."

After making a cursory examination of the ship Uncle Naboth received the Captain's report of what had transpired in his absence, and then we rowed back to town again.

We strolled through the city streets for an hour, had

supper, and then my uncle took me to his room, carefully closed and locked the door, and announced that he was ready to "talk business."

"Bein' partners," he said, "we've got to consult together; but I take it you won't feel bad, Sam, if I do most of the consultin'. I went down East to Batteraft to talk my plans with your father, but he slipped his cable an' I've got to talk 'em to you. If you see I'm wrong, anywhere, jest chip in an' stop me; but otherwise the less you say the more good we'll get out'n this 'ere conference."

"Very well, sir."

"To start in with, we've got a ship, an' a crew, an' plenty o' loose money. So what'll we do with 'em? Our business is to trade, an' to invest our money so we'll make more with it. What's the best way to do that?"

He seemed to pause for an answer, so I said: "I don't know sir."

"Nobody *knows*, of course. But we can guess, and then find out afterward if we've guessed right. All business is a gamble; and, if it wasn't, most men would quit an' go fishin'. After I got back from Japan I met a lot o' fellows that had been to Alaska huntin' gold. Seems like Alaska's full of gold, an' before long the whole country'll be flockin' there like sheep. All 'Frisco's gettin' excited about the thing, so they tell me, and if fortunes is goin' to be made in Alaska, we may as well speak for one ourselves."

"But we are not miners, Uncle; and it's bitter cold up there, they say."

"Well put. We'll let the crowds mine the gold, and then hand it over to us."

"I'm afraid I don't understand," said I, weakly.

"No call for you to try, Sam. I'm your guardeen, an' so I'll do the understandin' for us both. Folks has to eat, my lad, an' gold hunters is usually too excited to make proper provisions fer their stomachs. They're goin' to be mighty hungry out in Alaska, before long, an' when a man's hungry he'll pay liberal fer a square meal. Let's give it to him, Sam, an' take the consequences—which is gold dust an' nuggets."

"How will you do it, Uncle Nabe?"

"Load the 'Flipper' with grub an' carry it to Kipnac, or up the Yukon as far as Fort Weare, or wherever the gold fields open up. Then, when the miners get hungry, they'll come to us and trade their gold for our groceries. We're sure to make big profits, Sam."

"It looks like a reasonable proposition, sir," I said. "But it seems to me rather dangerous. Suppose our ship gets frozen in the ice, and we can't get away? And suppose about that time we've sold out our provisions. We can't eat gold. And suppose——"

"S'pose the moon falls out'n the sky," interrupted Uncle Naboth, "wouldn't it be dark at night, though!"

"Well, sir?"

"If the gold-diggers can live in the ice fields, we can live in a good warm ship. And we'll keep enough grub for ourselves, you may be sure of that."

47

"When do we start?" I asked, feeling sure that no arguments would move my uncle to abandon the trip, once he had made up his mind to undertake it.

"As soon as we can get the cargo aboard. It's coming on warmer weather, now, and this is the best time to make the voyage. A steamer left today with three hundred prospectors, an' they'll be goin' in bunches every day, now. Already I estimate there's over a thousand in the fields, so we won't get there any too soon to do business. What do you say, Sam?"

"I've nothing to say, sir. Being my guardian, you've decided the matter for both the partners, as is right and proper. As your clerk and assistant, I'll obey whatever orders you give me."

"That's the proper spirit, lad!" he cried, with enthusiasm. "We'll go to work tomorrow morning; and if all goes well we'll be afloat in ten days, with a full cargo!"

CHAPTER V.
"NUX" AND "BRYONIA."

On the seventh day of May, 1897, the "Flipper" weighed anchor and sailed before a light breeze through the Golden Gate and away on her voyage toward Alaska and its gold fields. Stored within her hold was a vast quantity of provisions of the sort that could be kept indefinitely without danger of spoiling. Flour, hams, bacon, sugar and coffee were represented; but canned meats and vegetables, tobacco and cheap cigars comprised by far the greater part of the cargo. Uncle Naboth had been seriously advised to carry a good supply of liquors, but refused positively to traffic in such merchandise.

Indeed, my uncle rose many degrees in my respect after I had watched for a time his preparations for our voyage. Simple, rough and uneducated he might be, but a shrewder man at a bargain I have never met in all my experience. And his reputation for honesty was so well established that his credit was practically unlimited among the wholesale grocers and notion jobbers of San Francisco. Everyone seemed ready and anxious to assist him, and the amount of consideration he met with on every hand was really wonderful.

"We've bought the right stuff, Sam," he said to me, as we stood on the deck and watched the shore gradually recede, "and now we've got to sell it right. That's the secret of good tradin'."

I was glad enough to find myself at sea, where I could rest from my labors of the past two weeks. I had been upon the docks night and day, it seemed, checking off packages of goods as fast as they were loaded on the lighters, and being unaccustomed to work I tired very easily. But my books were all accurate and "ship-shape," and I had found opportunity to fit up my little state-room with many comforts. In this I had been aided by Uncle Naboth, who was exceedingly liberal in allowing me money for whatever I required. At one time I said I would like to buy a few books, and the next day, to my surprise, he sent to my room a box containing the complete works of Walter Scott and Robert Louis Stevenson, with a miscellaneous collection of volumes by standard authors.

"I don't know much about books myself, Sam," he said; "so I got a feller that *does* know to pick 'em out for me, an' I guess you'll find 'em the right sort."

I did not tell him that I would have preferred to make my own selection, and afterward I frankly admitted to myself that the collection was an admirable one.

By this time I had come to know all the officers and crew, and found them a pretty good lot, taken altogether. The principle "characters" aboard were the dismal Captain Gay, who was really as contented a man as I ever knew, Acker, the ship's doctor, and two queer black men called by everybody Nux and Bryonia. Acker was a big, burly Englishman, who, besides being doctor, served as mate. He was jolly and good natured as the day was long, and had a few good stories which he told over and over again, invariably laughing at them more heartily than his auditors did. Singularly enough, Captain Gay and "Doc" Acker were close friends and cronies, and lived together in perfect harmony.

The black men interested me greatly from the moment I first saw them. Bryonia, or "Bry," as he was more frequently called, was the cook, and gave perfect satisfaction in that capacity. "Nux" was man-of-all-work, serving the cabin mess, assisting the cook, and acting as "able seaman" whenever required. He proved competent in nearly all ways, and was a prime favorite with officers and men.

They were natives of some small island of the Sulu archipelago, and their history was a strange one. In answer to my question as to why the blacks were so queerly named, Uncle Naboth related the following:

"It were six years ago, or thereabout, as we were homeward bound from our third Australy trip, that we sighted a native canoe in the neighborhood of the Caroline Islands. It was early in the mornin', and at first the lookout thought the canoe was empty; but it happened to lay in our course, and as we overtook it we saw two niggers lyin' bound in the bottom of the boat. So we lay to, an' picked 'em up, an' when they was histed aboard they were considerable more dead ner alive. Bill Acker was our mate then, as he is now, an' in his early days he studied to be a hoss doctor. So he always carries a box of medicines with him, to fix up the men in case they gets the jaundice or the colic. Mostly they's pills, an' sugar coated, for Doc hates to tackle drugs as is very dangerous. An' on account of a good deal of sickness among the crew that trip, an' consequently a good deal of experimentin' by Doc on

51

the medicine chest, the pills an' such like was nearly used up, though no one seemed much the worse for it.

"Well, after we'd cut the niggers' bonds, an' rubbed 'em good to restore the circulation, we come near decidin' they was dead an' heavin' of 'em overboard agin. But Doc wouldn't give up. He brought out the medicine box, an' found that all the stuff he had left was two bottles of pills, one of 'em Nux Vomica, an' the other Bryonia. I was workin' over one of the niggers, an' Doc he hands me one o' the bottles an says: 'Nux.' So I emptied the bottle into the dead man's mouth, an' by Jinks, Sam, he come around all right, and is alive an' kickin' today. Cap'n Gay dosed the other one with the Bryonia, an' it fetched him in no time. I won't swear it were the pills, you know; but the fact is the niggers lived.

"Afterwards we found the critters couldn't speak a word of English, ner tell us even what their names were. So we called one Nux, and the other Bryonia, accordin' to the medicine that had saved their lives, an' they've answered to those names ever since."

The blacks were gentle and good natured, and being grateful for their rescue they had refused to leave the ship at the end of the voyage, and were now permanent fixtures of the "Flipper."

"They are not slaves, are they?" I asked, when I had listened to this story.

"Mercy, no!" exclaimed Uncle Naboth. "They're as free as any of us, an' draw their wages reg'lar. Also they're as faithful as the day is long, an' never get drunk or mutinous. So it were a lucky day when we picked 'em up."

Bryonia stood fully six feet in height, and was muscular and wonderfully strong. He had a fine face, too, and large and intelligent eyes. Nux was much shorter, and inclined to be fat. But he was not a bit lazy, for all that, and accomplished an immense amount of work in so cheerful a manner that never a complaint was laid at his door. Not a sailor could climb aloft with more agility or a surer foot, and both Nux and Bryonia were absolutely fearless in the face of danger.

Although these men were black they were not negroes, but belonged to a branch of the Malay race. Their hair was straight, their noses well formed and their eyes very expressive and intelligent. The English they had picked up from the crew, however, was spoken with an accent not unlike that peculiar to the African negroes, but with a softer and more sibilant tone.

Before I had been on the ship a week both Nux and Bry were my faithful friends and devoted followers, and in the days that were to come their friendship and faithfulness stood me in good stead.

A very interesting person to me was big Bill Acker, the mate, called by courtesy "Doc." He seemed far above his mates in the matter of intelligence, and was evidently a well bred man in his youth. A shelf above his bunk bore a well-thumbed row of volumes on the world's great religions, together with a Talmud, a Koran, a Bible, the works of Confucius and Max Müller's translation of the Vedas. One seemed to have been as thoroughly read as the others, yet never have I heard Doc Acker say one word, good or bad, about religion. Whatever the result of his studies might be, he kept his opinions strictly to himself.

A stiff breeze sprang up during the first night, and the second day at sea found me miserably ill, and regretting that I had ever trusted myself to the mercies of cruel old ocean. Indeed, I lay in a most pitiable plight until the big Englishman came to me with doses of medicines from his chest. He might have been merely "a hoss doctor," as Uncle Naboth had said; but certain it is that his remedies helped me, and within twenty-four hours I was again able to walk the deck in comfort.

Perhaps I had inherited some of my father's fondness for salt water, for my new life soon became vastly interesting to me, and it was not long before I felt entirely at home on the dingy old "Flipper."

One morning, after standing by the bulwarks for a time watching the water slip by, I climbed upon the rail and sat with my heels dangling over the side. Suddenly I felt a strong hand grasp my shoulder and draw me to the deck, and I turned around indignantly to find black Nux beside me.

"Bad place to sit, Mars Sam," he said, coolly; "might tum'le ov'bode."

Before I could reply, Uncle Naboth, who had witnessed the incident, strolled up to us and said:

"Nux is right, my lad. You never find a sailor sitting on the rail; they know too well how onreliable the motion of a ship is. If anybody drops overboard the chances o' bein' picked up alive is mighty slim, I tell you. Only fools put 'emselves into unnecessary danger, Sam. Take it on them orful railroad cars, for instance. Old travellers always wait 'till the train stops afore they gets on or off the cars. Them as don't know the danger is the ones that gets hurt. Same way handlin' a gun. An old hunter once told me he never p'inted a gun at anything he didn't want to kill; but there's a lot o' folks killed ev'ry year that don't know the blamed thing is loaded. It ain't cowardly to be keerful, lad; but only fools an' ignorant people is reckless enough to get careless."

I am glad to say I took this lecture with good humor, admitting frankly that Uncle Naboth was right. At least once in the future a recollection of this caution saved me from hopeless disaster.

On the sixth day the breeze died away and the ship lay still. There was not a breath of air, and the heat was so intense that the interior of the ship was like a furnace. At night we slept upon the deck, and by day we lay gasping beneath the shade of the tarpaulins. Bryonia let the galley fire die out and served us cold lunches, but our appetites were small.

There being no occasion to work, the crew gathered in little bunches and told a series of never-ending yarns that were very interesting to me, because most of them were of hair-breadth adventures and escapes that were positively wonderful—if one tried to believe them. One of the best of these story-tellers was Ned Britton, who had been appointed our boatswain and was already popular with his mates. As his yarns were all of the Atlantic, and most of the "Flipper's" crew had sailed only on the Pacific, Britton opened to them a new field of adventures, which met with universal approval.

Nux and Bry, who bore the heat better than their white brethren, added to the general amusement by giving exhibitions of the Moro war dances, ending with desperate encounters, with sticks to represent spears, that were sure to arouse the entire crew to enthusiasm. They sometimes sang their native war songs, also—a series of monotonous, guttural chants. And then Dan Donnegan, a little, red-whiskered Irishman, would wind up with "Bryan O'Lynne" or some other comic ditty that set the forecastle roaring with laughter.

During this period of enforced idleness the dismal Captain Gay walked the deck with solemn patience and watched for signs of a breeze. Bill Acker, the mate, read his religious library all through—probably for the hundredth time. Uncle Nabe taught me cribbage, and we played for hours at a time, although I usually came out second best at the game. Also I learned the ropes of the ship and received many lessons in navigation from my friends the sailors, not one of whom knew anything about that abstruse problem.

"Thay ain't a man o' the lot as could take the ship back to 'Frisco, in case of emergency," said my uncle; and I believe he was right. Common sailors are singularly ignorant of navigation, although they have a way of deceiving themselves into thinking they know all about it.

After being becalmed six days, the intense heat was at last relieved by a thin breeze, which sprung up during the night. The sails were at once trimmed, and within an hour the "Flipper" was skipping the little waves to the satisfaction of all on board.

But the wind steadily increased, and by morning all hands were called to shorten sail. By noon we encountered a stiff gale, which blew from the east, and soon lashed the waves into a mad frenzy.

As the storm gradually increased Captain Gay began to look anxious. There was a brief lull toward evening, during which a great hail-storm descended upon us, the icy bullets pelting the sailors unmercifully and driving all to shelter. Then the wind redoubled its fury, and the Captain put the ship before it, allowing the gale to bear us considerably out of our course.

Uncle Naboth growled considerably at this necessity, but he did not interfere in the least with Captain Gay's management of the ship. Safety was more important to us than time, and Gay was not a man to take unnecessary chances.

The three wild days that followed have always seemed to me since like a horrible dream. I had no idea a ship could be so tossed and pounded and battered about, and still live. It was a mere chip on the great, angry ocean, and the water washed our decks almost continually. After one of these deluges, when every man strove to save himself by clinging to the life lines, two of our best sailors were missed, and we never saw them again. Uncle Nabe began to whistle, and every time he saw me he gave one of his humorous winks or fell to chuckling in his silent way; but my white face could not have been much encouragement to gaiety, and I believe he was not over merry himself, but merely trying to cheer me up.

But, although the danger was so imminent, not a man flinched or gave way to fear, and Nux and Bryonia performed their duties as calmly as if the sea were smooth. The vessel was staunch enough, so far; but it pitched and tossed so violently that even burly Doc Acker was obliged to crawl into the cabin on his hands and knees to get his meals.

We fled before the wind until the third night, when the rudder chain broke and the helmsman was thrown, crushed and bleeding, against the lee bulwarks. The "Flipper," released from all control, swung quickly around, and the big mainmast snapped like a pipe-stem and came tumbling with its cordage to the decks, where our brave sailors rushed upon it and cut it clear. I thought the ship would never right again, after the careening given it by the fallen mast; but, somehow, it did, and morning found us still afloat, although badly crippled and at the mercy of the waves.

As if satisfied with the havoc it had wrought, the gale now abated; but the waves ran high for another forty-eight hours, and our crew could do nothing but cling to the remaining rigging and await calmer weather.

Fortunately our ballast and cargo held in place through all, and the hull showed no sign of a leak. When the sea grew calmer we floated upright upon the water and it was found our straits were not nearly so desperate as we had feared.

Yet our condition was serious enough to make me wonder what was to become of us. The rudder had been entirely washed away; the mainmast was gone;

the mizzenmast had broken at the head and the foresail royals were in splinters. All the deck was cumbered with rigging; the starboard bulwarks had been stove in by the fallen mast, and our crew was lessened by three able seamen.

But Captain Gay, no less dismal than before, you may be sure, promptly began to issue orders, and the men fell to with a will to repair the damage as best they might. First they rigged up a temporary rudder and swung it astern. It was a poor makeshift, however, and only with good weather could we hope it would steer us to the nearest port.

While the men cleared the decks and rigged up a jury mast under the supervision of the mate, Captain Gay took our bearings and ascertained that we had not departed so greatly from our course as we had feared. Yet it was impossible to make the mouth of the Yukon in our present condition, or even to reach a shelter in Bering Sea. It was found, however, that the Alaska peninsula was not far away, so we decided to draw as near to that as possible, in the hope of meeting a passing vessel or finding a temporary refuge on some one of the numerous islands that lie in this part of the North Pacific.

For four days we labored along, in our crippled condition, without sighting land; but then our fortunes changed. During the night a good breeze from the southwest swept us merrily along, and when daylight came we found ourselves close to a small, wooded island. It lay in the form of a horse-shoe, with a broad, protected bay in the center, and Captain Gay, anxious to examine his ship more closely, decided at once to enter the harbor and cast anchor.

This was by no means an easy task, for long lines of reefs extended from each point of the shore, almost enclosing the bay with jagged rocks. But the sea was calm and the position of the reefs clearly marked; so that by skillful maneuvering the "Flipper" passed between them in safety, and to the relief and satisfaction of all on board we dropped our anchor in the clear waters of the bay.

CHAPTER VI.
THE LAND OF MYSTERY.

Captain Gay examined his chart with minute care, and solemnly shook his head.

The island was not there. Either the chart was imperfect, or we had reached a hitherto undiscovered land. The latter conjecture was not at all unreasonable, for so many islands lay in this neighborhood that even when sighted by chance an outlying islet was little liable to tempt one to land upon it. This was doubtless one of the numerous group lying to the south-east of the Alaska peninsula, which are of volcanic origin and as a rule barren and uninhabited.

I have said this island was well wooded, but not until we were opposite the mouth of the natural harbor did we observe this fact. From the sea only a line of rugged headlands and peaks showed plainly, and had we not been in distress we should never have thought to stop at this place. Once within the harbor, however, the scene that met our view was not unattractive.

Bordering the bay was a sandy beach a full hundred yards in width, broken only by an inlet toward the left, or south, which seemed to lead into the interior of the island, winding between high and precipitous banks and soon becoming lost to sight. Back of the beach was the clean-cut edge of a forest, not following a straight line, but rising and falling in hills and ravines until it seemed from the bay to have been

61

scalloped into shape by a pair of huge scissors. The woods were thick and the trees of uniform size, and between them grew a mass of vines and underbrush that made them almost impenetrable. How far the forest extended we were unable to guess; nor did we know how wide the island might be, for back of the hills rose a range of wooded mountains nearly a thousand feet in height, and what might lie beyond these was of course a matter of conjecture. Uncle Naboth, however, advanced the opinion that the island ended at the mountain peaks, and dropped sheer down to the sea beyond. He had seen many formations of that sort, and supposed we had found the only possible harbor on the island.

There was no apparent indication that the island had ever before been visited by man. Even signs of native occupation were lacking. But Captain Gay decided to send a small boat ashore to explore the inlet before we could relax all vigilance and feel that we were not liable to attack or interruption.

So the gig was lowered, and four of the crew, accompanied by Bill Acker, the mate, set off upon their voyage of discovery. They rowed straight to the inlet, which proved to be navigable, and soon after entering it we lost sight of the boat as it wound between the wooded cliffs.

We waited patiently an hour; two hours; three hours; but the boat did not return. Then patience gave way to anxiety, and finally the suspense became unbearable. After the loss of our three sailors during the storm we were reduced to eleven men, besides Uncle Naboth and myself, who were not counted members of the crew. Thirteen on board was not an especially lucky number, so that some of the men had been looking for disaster of some sort ever since we sighted the island. Those now remaining on the "Flipper" were the Captain, Ned Britton and two other sailors, Nux and Bryonia, my Uncle and myself; eight, all told. To send more men after the five who were absent would be to reduce our numbers more than was wise; yet it was impossible for us to remain inactive. Finally, Ned Britton offered to attempt to make his way through the woods, along the edge of the inlet, and endeavor to find out what had become of Acker and his men. He armed himself with two revolvers and a stout cutlass, and then we rowed him to the shore and watched him start on his expedition.

Not expecting that Ned would be long absent, we did not at once return to the ship. Instead, the Captain backed the boat into deep water and lay to, that we might pick up our messenger when he reappeared.

It had been agreed that if Ned came upon the mate he was to fire two shots in quick succession, to let us know that all was well. If he encountered danger he was to fire a single shot. If he wished us to come to his assistance he would fire three shots. But the afternoon passed slowly and quietly, and no sound of any kind came from the interior to relieve our anxiety. The boat returned to the ship, and Bryonia served our supper amid an ominous and gloomy silence on the part of those few who were left.

There was something uncanny about this mysterious disappearance of our comrades. Had they been able to return or to communicate with us there was no doubt they would have done so; therefore their absence was fraught with unknown but no less certain

63

terror. Big Bill Acker was a man of much resource, and absolutely to be depended upon; and Ned Britton, who had been fully warned and would be on his guard against all dangers, was shrewd and active and not liable to be caught napping.

What, then, had they encountered? Wild beasts, savages, or some awful natural phenomenon which had cruelly destroyed them? Our imaginations ran riot, but it was all imagination, after all, and we were no nearer the truth.

An anxious night passed, and at daybreak Uncle Naboth called a council of war, at which all on board were present. We faced a hard proposition, you may be sure, for not one of us had any information to guide him, and all were alike in the dark.

To desert our absent friends and sail away from the island was impossible, even had we desired to do so; for our numbers were too small to permit us to work the disabled "Flipper" in safety, and the ship's carpenter, on whom we greatly depended, had gone with the mate. All repairs must be postponed until the mystery of the men's disappearance was solved; and we firmly resolved that those of us remaining must not separate, but stick together to the last, and stick to the ship, as well.

Good resolutions, indeed; but we failed to consider the demands of an aroused curiosity. After two days had dragged their hours away without a sign of our absent comrades human nature could bear the suspense no longer.

Uncle Naboth called another council, and said:

"Boys, we're actin' like a pack o' cowards. Let's follow after our friends, an' find 'em, dead or alive. We oughtn't to shrink from a danger we sent 'em into; and if we can't rescue 'em, let's run the chance of dyin' with 'em."

This sentiment met with general approval. All felt that the time for action had arrived, and if there was a reluctant man among us he made no sign.

Early next morning we partook of a hasty breakfast and then tumbled into the long boat to begin our quest. Every one on the ship was to accompany the expedition, for no one cared to be left behind. Uncle Naboth at first proposed to leave me on board, in the care of Bry; but I pleaded hard to go with the rest, and it was evident that I would be in as much danger aboard as in the company of the exploring party. So it was decided to take me along, and we practically deserted the ship, taking with us a fair supply of provisions and plenty of ammunition. The men were fully armed, and my uncle even intrusted me with a revolver, for I had learned to shoot fairly well.

It was a beautiful morning, cool and fresh and sunny, as we rowed away from the ship and headed for the inlet. That unknown and perhaps terrible dangers lay ahead of us we had good reason to expect; but every man was alert and vigilant and eager to unravel the mystery of this strange island.

CHAPTER VII.
THE MAJOR.

Presently we shot into the opening and passed swiftly up the smooth waters of the inlet. The hills were gradually sloping, at first, and we could look into the tangled mass of forest that lay on either hand. But soon the sides of the channel became rocky and precipitous, rising higher and higher until we found ourselves in a deep gorge that wound between gigantic overhanging cliffs. The waters of the inlet were still smooth, but it narrowed perceptibly, all the time curving sharply to the right and then to the left in a series of zig-zags; so that every few minutes we seemed to be approaching a solid rocky wall, which suddenly disclosed a continuation of the channel to right angles with it, allowing us to continue on our course.

It was indeed necessary to watch out, in such a place as this, for we were passing through the heart of the mountain, and could not tell from one moment to another what lay before us.

There was barely room on each side for the sweep of the oars, so that we had to pull straight and carefully; but after a time the deep gloom in which we were engulfed began to lighten, and we were aware that the slope of the mountain was decreasing, and we were approaching its further side.

On and on we rowed, twisting abruptly this way and that, until suddenly, as we turned a sharp corner and shot into open, shallow water, the adventure culminated in a mighty surprise.

We were surrounded by a band of men—big, brawny fellows who stood waist deep in the water and threw coils of rope about us before we were quite aware of their presence. At the same time they caught the boat and arrested its progress, jerking the oars from the hands of our rowers and making us fast prisoners.

Only Bryonia was quicker than the men who sought to entrap him. Before the noose could settle over his shoulders he leaped into the air and dove headlong beneath the water. But the brave attempt to escape was all in vain, for as he rose to the surface a dozen hands caught him and drew him to the shore, where, despite his struggles, he was bound as securely as the rest of us.

So unexpected was the attack and so cleverly were we mastered that scarcely a word was uttered by our little party as we stared in astonishment into the rough and bearded faces of our captors. Only Captain Gay muttered a string of naughty words under his breath; the rest were silent, and Uncle Naboth, bound round and round with rope so that he could not move, sat in his seat and looked across at me with one of his quaintest winks, as if he would cheer me up in this unexpected crisis.

Nor had a word been spoken by the men who entrapped us. Wading slowly through the water, they drew our boat to a sandy shore and beached it, while we looked curiously around upon the scene that was now clearly unfolded to our view.

The cliffs had ended abruptly, and the center of the island, flat and broad, lay stretched before us. The waters of the inlet from here became shallow, and a wide beach of strangely bright sands extended for two hundred feet on either side of it. Then came the jungle, thick and seemingly impenetrable, beyond which all was unknown. Straight and without a ripple the water lay before as a full quarter of a mile, disappearing thence into the forest.

On the thick sands of the east shore, where we now were, a number of rude huts had been erected, shaped something like Indian tepees and made of intertwined branches covered with leaves from the forest. These stood in a row near to the edge of the jungle, so as to take advantage of its shade.

But more strange than all this was the appearance of the men who had bound us. They were evidently our own countrymen, and from their dress and manners seemed to be miners. But nearly all were in rags and tatters, as if they had been long away from civilization, and their faces were fierce and brutal, bearing the expression of wild beasts in search of prey.

One of them, however, who stood upon the beach regarding us silently and with folded arms, was a personage so remarkable that he instantly riveted our attention. His height was enormous—at least six feet and three inches—and his chest was broad and deep as that of ancient Hercules. He was bearded like a gorilla with fiery red hair, which extended even to his great chest, disclosed through the open grey flannel shirt. There was no hat upon his head, and he wore no coat; but high boots were upon his feet and around his waist a leathern belt stuck full of knives and revolvers.

No stage pirate, no bandit of Southern Europe, was ever half so formidable in appearance as this terrible personage. He stood motionless as a pillar of stone, but his little red eyes, quick and shrewd, roved from one to another of our faces, as if he were making a mental estimate of each one of us—like the ogre who selected his fattest prisoner to grace his pot-pie.

I own that I shuddered as his glance fell upon me; and we were all more or less disquieted by our rough seizure and the uncertainty of the fate that awaited us.

This man—the red giant—was undoubtedly the leader of the outlaw band, for having pulled our boat upon the beach and dragged Bryonia to a position beside it, all eyes were turned enquiringly upon him.

He strode forward a few steps, fixed his eyes firmly upon Uncle Naboth, and said:

"Did you leave anyone aboard the ship?"

I gave a start of surprise. The voice of the huge bandit was as gentle and soft as that of a woman.

"No," said my uncle.

"I guess, Major, we've got 'em all now," remarked one of the men.

The giant nodded and turned again to Uncle Naboth.

"You must pardon us, sir, for our seeming rudeness," said he, with a politeness that seemed absolutely incongruous, coming from his coarse, hairy lips. "My men and I are in desperate straights, and only desperate remedies will avail to save us. I beg you all to believe that we have no personal enmity toward you whatever." Then he turned to his men, and with a wave of his hand added: "Bring them along."

Captured by the gold-hunters.

Thereat we were jerked from our seats in the boat and led away over the sands toward the edge of the jungle. I noticed that our arms and provisions, being confiscated, were carried into one of the huts, but we ourselves were dragged past these and through an opening in the trees just large enough to admit us single file.

A few steps from the edge we entered a circular clearing, perhaps a dozen paces in diameter, hemmed in on all sides by a perfect network of tangled brushwood and vines. Here, to our great joy, we came upon our lost comrades, all seated at the base of slender trees, to which they were bound by stout ropes.

"Hurrah!" cried Bill Acker, a smile lighting his careworn face. "It's a joy to see you again, my boys, although you seem to have fallen into the same trap we did."

"Beg parding, Cap'n, for getting myself caught," said Net Britton, quite seriously. "The brutes jumped me so quick I hadn't time to fire a shot."

"All right, Ned; you're not to blame," said Captain Gay, and while we were interchanging greetings our captors were busily engaged in securing us to trees, in the same manner the others were bound. We protested, very naturally, at such treatment, but the men, surly and rough, answered us not a word, and after making sure we could not get away they withdrew and left us alone.

As the trees to which we were fastened were at the edge of the clearing we were seated in a sort of circle, facing one another.

"Well, boys," said Uncle Naboth, "here's a pretty kettle o' fish, I must say! The whole crew o' the 'Flipper,' officers an' men an' supercargo, has been caught like so many turtles, an' turned on their backs; an' all we can do is to kick and wish we had our legs agin."

We all seemed rather ashamed of ourselves. Captain Gay heaved a most dismal sigh, and turning to Acker asked:

"Who are these people, Bill?"

"Can't say, I'm sure, Tom. We rowed up the inlet, not expecting any danger, when suddenly the whole lot jumped us and made us prisoners in the wink of an eye. They brought us before a red devil called the Major, who pumped us to find out how many men were aboard ship. When we refused to give them any information they brought us to this place, and here we've been ever since, fast bound and half starved, for I guess the fellows haven't much to eat themselves."

"How did they come here?" asked my uncle.

"Really, sir," replied Acker, "they haven't told us one word about themselves."

"Fer my part," said Ned Britton, speaking in his deliberate manner, "I think these pirates has been spyin' on us ever since we anchored in the bay. They must have a path over the mountains that we don't know of, for when the mate come up the inlet in the gig they was ready an' waitin' for him, and he didn't have a chance to resist. 'Twere the same with me, sir. I crep' along the edge o' the channel, goin' slow an' swingin' myself from tree to tree over the gulch—for the trees was too thick to get between 'em—until I come to this here place, where two men grabbed me an knocked me down an' tied me up like a pig sent to market. The Major were with 'em, and swore he'd murder me if I didn't tell him how many more were aboard the ship, an' what her cargo was, an' where we are bound for, an' a dozen other things. But I kep' mum, sir, as were my duty, an' finally they brung me to this place, where I was mighty glad to find the mate and his men safe and sound."

We then related our own anxiety over the fate of those who had so mysteriously disappeared, and our final expedition in search of them.

"We've found you, all right," said Uncle Naboth, in conclusion; "but now the question is, what's goin' to become of us, an' what shall we do to escape from these blamed pirates that's captured us?"

"Before you answer that question," said a quiet voice, "it may be as well for you to listen to what I have to say."

We looked up and saw the great form of the Major standing in the clearing. How much of our conversation he had overheard we did not know; but after a lowering glance into our startled faces he calmly seated himself in the midst of the circle.

"Thirteen, all told," he said. "You seem shorthanded, for so big a schooner."

"We lost three men in the storm," said Uncle Naboth.

"What are you, the owner?" asked the Major.

"Part owner."

"What is your cargo?"

"Mixed," replied Uncle Naboth, non-committally.

The Major reflected a moment.

"We shall soon find out all we wish to know," he said. "We have both your boats, and we can examine the ship for ourselves."

"I s'pose you know this is a hangin' matter?" suggested my uncle.

"It may be," was the calm reply. "At any rate, it is illegal, and I regret that circumstances force us to act illegally with you. As a matter of fact, I wish that I might have treated you with more courtesy. But you had no business to come to this island, and having come here, and surprised our great secret by penetrating into the center of the land, you must take the consequences of your folly. We did not want you here, and we kept out of your way as long as you would let us. When you invaded our private domain we were forced to protect ourselves."

"I don't understand," said my uncle, much puzzled by this speech. "We're no robbers, ner pirates. We're peaceful, citizens of the United States."

"So are we," retorted the Major. "But we're also the creatures of fate, and our condition here forces us to wage warfare upon any who intrude into our privacy."

"We put in here for repairs, an' it was natural we should want to explore the island," returned my uncle, doggedly.

The Major appeared lost in thought. For several minutes he sat staring at the ground with a great frown wrinkling his brow. For our part, we watched him curiously, wondering the while what would be the outcome of the queer condition in which we found ourselves. Finally the man spoke:

"Under the circumstances," said he, "there are but two courses open to us. One is to murder every man of you, and bury you underneath the sands. I imagine you would be safe there, and not a soul on earth would ever know what had become of you."

I shuddered. The soft tones could not disguise the horror of the words.

"The alternative," continued the Major, "is to swear you to secrecy, to induce you to work for us for fair wages, and finally to sail back with you in your ship to San Francisco, where we may part good friends."

The contrast between these propositions was so great that we stared at the man in amazement.

"If we are to take our choice," said Uncle Naboth, "it won't be the grave under the sands, you may be sure."

"The choice does not lie with you, but with my men," returned the Major, coolly. "For my part, I am neither bloodthirsty nor inclined to become a murderer; so I shall use my influence in your behalf."

With this he slowly rose to his feet and stalked from the clearing, leaving us to reflections that were not entirely comfortable.

The hours passed drearily enough. Toward evening

some of the men brought us a few moldy ship's biscuits and a bucket of sweet drinking water, and after partaking of this we were left to ourselves until the next daybreak.

As it grew dusk Nux suddenly rose from his seat, and we saw that he was free. In some way he had managed to slip his bonds, and he passed quickly from one to another of us until we were all released from the dreadful ropes that had been chafing us.

Then a council of war was held. Our captors numbered about thirty, and all were fully armed. To attempt to oppose them openly would be madness; but if we could manage to slip away and regain our boats we should be able to reach our ship and so escape. Bryonia agreed to spy out our surroundings and see where the boats lay, so he fell upon all fours and silently crept from the clearing.

We awaited his return with impatience, but he was not gone long. He re-entered the clearing walking upright and indifferent to crackling twigs, and then we knew our case was hopeless.

"Dere's men sleepin' in de boats, an' men on watch," said he; "an' dey all has swords an' pistols. Can't get away anyhow, Mars Perkins."

"How about the woods?" asked my uncle. "Can't we escape through them?"

Bry shook his head, decisively. He was an expert woodsman, and declared no man could penetrate the thick jungle that hemmed us in. Ned Britton also bore testimony to this fact; so we were obliged to sadly abandon any hope of escape, and stretched ourselves as comfortably as we might upon the ground to await the approach of morning.

With the first streaks of day the Major and a dozen of his men arrived, and without appearing to notice that we had slipped our bonds they drove us in a pack from the clearing and out upon the sands that bordered the inlet.

Here we saw others of our captors busy preparing breakfast before the entrances to the rude huts, and it was evident that they were using the provisions they had captured from us, for I scented the aroma of the coffee that Uncle Naboth was so proud of, and carried with him wherever he went.

We gathered before the hut of the Major, which was somewhat larger than the others, and then the leader said, in a tone of stern command: "Take off your clothes."

We hesitated, not quite understanding the purpose of the order.

"Strip, my boys," said another of the pirates, with a grin. "We want your togs. We drew cuts for 'em last night, and now we'll trade you our rags for 'em."

So we stripped and tossed our clothes upon the ground, where they were eagerly seized by the outlaws and donned with great satisfaction. The Major did not participate in this robbery; but, indeed, no garment that we wore could possibly have fitted his huge frame.

When we had put on the rags discarded by the

others we were a curious looking lot, you may be sure. Uncle Naboth had a fit of silent merriment at my expense, but if he could have seen himself I am sure he would have choked and sputtered dangerously. A more disreputable appearance than that we now presented would be hard to imagine; but our enemies did not profit so greatly by the exchange, after all, for the garments fitted them as badly as theirs did us. However, they seemed very proud of their acquisition, and strutted around like so many vain peacocks.

CHAPTER VIII.
THE SANDS OF GOLD.

The sun had now arisen and flooded the scene with its glorious rays. We were given some of the coffee and a scant allowance of food for our breakfast, the care with which the latter was doled out being evidence that our captors did not know that the "Flipper" was loaded down with provisions.

As soon as the meal was concluded we all gathered around the Major's hut again, and he began to make us an address.

"At the conference held last evening," he began, in his smooth tone, "we decided to allow you to choose your own fate. It is death on the one hand, and life as our paid employees on the other. What do you say?"

"We'd like to know, sir," said Uncle Naboth, "what you are doing on this island?"

"Washing gold."

"Gold!"

"To be sure," said the Major. "Are you so ignorant that you cannot see that these sands upon which you are standing are wonderfully rich in gold?"

"Why, I hadn't noticed," said my uncle, and then we all curiously stared at the bright billows of sand that filled the beach on both sides of the inlet.

"It will do no harm to explain to you how we came here, and what we are doing," said the Major. "It will help you to make your decision."

"Seems like a queer place to look for gold," said Uncle Naboth, reflectively. "But even then I can't see why you've treated us like you have, or why you're so blamed secret about the thing."

"Can't you?" was the reply. "Then I must jog your reason with a few sensible suggestions. Every gold field yet discovered has been a magnet to draw men from every part of the civilized world. The result has been that the first discoverers seldom profit to any extent, while the horde they draw around them get the lion's share. That has been our experience time and time again, for every member of our band is an experienced miner. We've been crowded from Colorado to Idaho, from Idaho to California, from California to the Black Hills, and back again. Finally we got word of a rich find of gold in Alaska; so, banding together, we chartered an old ship and started for the Yukon. On the way we encountered a gale that blew us to this island. We don't know what island it is, and we don't care. While our vessel was undergoing repairs we rowed up the inlet, as you did, and discovered these sands, which are marvelously rich with grains of pure gold. Before your eyes, gentlemen, lies the greatest natural accumulation of gold the world has ever known."

He paused, after this impressive statement, and again we looked around wonderingly.

"We can't get it all, that's true," resumed the Major; "but we have decided to stay here and defend our

82

secret until each one of us has secured an independent fortune. Then the swarms of gold-hunters can settle here as thickly as they please. Of course we had our tools with us, and a good supply of provisions; so we were glad to let Alaska take care of itself and go to work washing out the wealth that lay at our feet. We knew the food wouldn't last till we were ready to leave here, so we decided to send the ship home for more provisions. The captain was bound to secrecy by promise of a big share for himself, but soon after he sailed away a great storm arose, and probably the old, leaky craft never weathered it, for that was over a year ago, and no ship has reached this harbor until yours appeared."

We listened to this recital with eager interest, for it explained much that had puzzled us. And Uncle Naboth remarked:

"It's a strange story, sir. But I don't see why you treated us as enemies when we came here."

"Suppose you had been prospectors, like ourselves. What would become of our secret then?"

"But we're not," was the reply.

"It was even possible our captain might have reached shore and betrayed us. In that case you might be the forerunners of an army of invaders. We couldn't take the chances, sir. We've been disappointed too many times. But it appears that you were merely the victims of the elements, and like ourselves were driven to this shore in a gale. So the only danger to be feared from you is your getting away before we're ready to go with you. That was why we hesitated between murdering you and using your services to enable us to accomplish our task sooner than we otherwise could. We are not cut-throats, believe me, nor do we care to be responsible for the death of so many decent men. But the lust for gold has made my fellows desperate, and with immense fortunes within their grasp they will stick at nothing to protect themselves and their treasure."

"That's only natural," growled Uncle Naboth.

"I'm glad to find you so reasonable," said the Major. "Having discovered this field ourselves, we do not intend to share the gold with anyone; but we will make you a reasonable proposition. We will pay each one of you two dollars a day, in grains of gold, for your labor, and you must buckle to and help us to get out the gold. We will also pay you, in gold, for whatever provisions you have on your ship, or other supplies we may need. And when we have enough to satisfy ourselves, and are ready to sail back to civilization, we will pay you a reasonable price for passage in your ship. That seems to me to be fair and square. What do you say?"

"Why," answered Uncle Naboth, with a gasp, "that's all we could look for if we got to Alaska. We're traders, sir, an' expect to make our money in trade. The only thing we object to is workin' like dogs to wash gold for somebody else."

"You'll have to put up with that objection," returned the man, dryly. "Your labor will shorten our stay here a full year, and it's the penalty you must suffer for being in our power."

My uncle turned to his crew.

"What do you say, boys?" he asked.

Some grumbled, and all looked grave; but a glance at the lowering faces of the miners assured them that discretion was the better part of valor, so they yielded a reluctant consent to the arrangement.

"There's one p'int, howsomever, as I should like to argufy," said Uncle Naboth. "This here lad's too small an' delicate to work at the washin', an' somebody's got to give out the provisions an' collect the pay for 'em. Let him out o' the deal, sir, an' make him clerk o' the supplies."

"I will agree to that," said the Major, promptly. "When we get back to the States we don't want to have anything against our record; so this bargain shall be kept faithfully on our side. I'll prepare a paper, which every man here must sign, stating that you accept the agreement freely and without compulsion, and will be satisfied with your wages and the payment for your groceries and supplies. Also you must each one take an oath not to betray to anyone the whereabouts of this island after you leave it, for it will be a valuable possession to us even after we've taken enough gold from it to make us rich. Meantime you'll be well treated, but carefully watched. To some extent you'll be, morally, our prisoners; but the only hardship you will suffer is to labor hard for a few months at a small salary."

"That's agreeable, sir," said my uncle; and the men accepted the arrangement with more or less grace.

Then the conference broke up. Our sailors, as well as Captain Gay, the mate and my uncle, were at once set to work washing gold on the banks of the inlet, their numbers being distributed among the miners, who showed them what to do and supervised the work. It appeared that all the gold gathered by our people was to go into a common pot, to be distributed equally among our captors; but each miner worked for himself alone, and was entitled to whatever he secured. In this way a premium was set upon individual industry, and they worked eagerly and persistently, at the same time insisting that the "Flipper's" crew did not loiter.

The Major, whose influence over his rough comrades was undoubted, retired within his tent to draft the paper we were to sign, and I, left to my own devices, wandered here and there, watching the men and wondering what would be the outcome of this singular adventure.

At noon the paper was ready, and it set forth clearly and fairly the terms of the agreement. We were all required to sign it, as well as every miner in the camp, and then the Major took possession of it, there being no duplicate.

After the midday meal six of our sailors were selected to man the long boat, and then accompanied by the Major, who was fully armed, and by myself, they rowed down the inlet to the harbor, and we boarded the ship.

I selected such of the provisions as were most needed by the half starved miners, and also carried away a number of blankets, as the nights were chill and the blankets would prevent much suffering.

Two trips we made that afternoon, and when the miners stopped work for the day I had quite a heap of groceries piled upon the sands. Instantly they surrounded me, clamoring for supplies, which I served to each man as he demanded them.

They paid me in grains of pure gold, which they drew from sacks, old stockings tied with a string, and even pockets cut from their clothing. How much to demand I did not know, and some paid me too much, I suppose, and some too little. One of them, a low browed, black bearded fellow called Larkin, obtained a quantity of goods and then said he would pay me some other time; but the Major insisted that I be paid then and there. So the man laid down a pinch of gold, saying it was enough, and I was about to accept it when the Major drew his revolver and said, quietly:

"This is a fair deal, Larkin. Shell out!"

The fellow uttered a string of angry oaths, but he added to his first offering until his leader was satisfied, and then went away vowing "to get even with the robbers."

To avoid further trouble, I brought a small pair of scales from the ship next day. They were not very accurate, I fear, but they were much better than guesswork. The Major and I figured out exactly what weight of gold should stand for a dollar, and I was allowed to put my own price on our supplies; but I took care not to be exorbitant in my demands, and most of the men expressed themselves as well satisfied with the arrangement.

As a good share of the provisions would suffer by

being left out in the night air, it was decided to build a warehouse for my use: "a reg'lar grocery store," Uncle Naboth described it; so the men all set to work, and under the direction of our ship's carpenter soon constructed a roomy and comfortable hut for this purpose. By repeated trips to the ship in the long boat, I soon accumulated a good stock of everything our cargo represented, and by taking off the covers of the boxes and then piling them on their edges, in rows, I soon made my hut look like a prosperous mercantile establishment. Surplus and unopened boxes were utilized to form a counter in front of my stock, and here I placed my scales and weighed the gold that was offered in payment.

The men were as prodigal as all miners are, and denied themselves nothing so long as they had gold to pay for it. So my stock gradually increased in gold and diminished in merchandise, and the men were well fed and comfortable.

But the sands upon which we so carelessly trod were wonderfully rich in the precious metal, and any sort of industry was sure to be repaid enormously by the glittering grains scattered about. It was not dust, you understand, but tiny grains resembling those of granulated sugar. The richest yield was derived from the sands at the bottom of the shallow inlet, and the practice of the miners was to wade a little way into the stream, scoop up a basin off the sandy bottom and wash it until only the specks of sparkling metal remained. As it was difficult to care for this properly, I brought from the ship a quantity of sail-cloth, which I made, during my leisure moments, into stout bags, about the size of salt-sacks, sewing the seams firmly.

These bags I sold readily to the miners, who, when they filled one, would usually bury it beneath the sand in their hut, so that it would be safe. I did not do this with my supply, however, but piled my sacks into an empty box in one corner of my grocery store, feeling sure there would be no theft of them in the confines of our little camp. Neither did the Major secrete his hoard, which lay plainly in sight of anyone who entered his hut; and the Major's store of gold was enormous because he took charge of all that our men washed out, until the time for final division should arrive.

There was no game of any sort, that we knew of, upon the island; but the men caught plenty of fish in the upper part of the inlet and in the bay upon the ocean frontage. The thickets surrounding our camp were considered absolutely impenetrable, on account of the underbrush and creeping vines that formed such a thick network at the foot of the trees. Yet there was a man named Daggett who, it was rumored, had found a way to traverse the forest with comparative ease.

This Daggett was quite a remarkable person, and enters now into my story.

He was a thin, withered little man, about fifty years of age who had been an unsuccessful miner all his life until now. So eager was he, at first, to take advantage of the great opportunities here afforded to secure a fortune, that he would work by moonlight washing gold, while his companions slept and rested from their labors. But soon he conceived an idea that these golden sands were deposited from some point in the mountains of the interior of the island, where solid gold abounded in enormous quantities. So he quit washing, and began a search for the imaginary "mountain of gold," cutting a secret path through the thicket to the more open interior, and passing day after day in his eager quest. At first he urged some of his comrades to join him, but they only laughed at his idea, being well content to obtain the coveted gold in an easy way, where it lay plainly before their eyes.

But Daggett did not desist, spending day after day in roaming through the wild hills in his fruitless search. During the time he lost in this way his mates were accumulating a vast store of golden grains, while Daggett was as yet only in possession of the result of his first eager labors; and after I opened my grocery store he was obliged to exchange pinches of his small substance for supplies, so that it gradually dwindled away to a mere nothing. He haggled so over the price of every article he secured that his fellows jeered him unmercifully, calling him "the miser" and berating him for neglecting his opportunities. Indeed, the poor fellow was well-nigh desperate, at the last, for he alone of all the camp was still poor, and his only salvation, he considered, was to find the hills of solid gold before the time came for all to abandon the island. So he was gone for days, returning to camp to secure provisions; and no one knew where he wandered or seem to care.

CHAPTER IX.
THE OUTLAWS.

There were many curious characters at the camp, as I suppose there are everywhere that a number of men are gathered together. I used to amuse myself studying the various phases of human nature that came under my observation, with the result that some men attracted me and some repelled me.

Aside from the miserly Daggett the man who caused me the most trouble was the surly, scowling Larkin, whom the Major had threatened to shoot on sight if he did not pay me for everything he obtained at my shop. He was a lazy fellow, and did not seem to get ahead as fast as his companions, for that reason. Sometimes, in the heat of the afternoon, he would strike work and come into my hut, where he threatened and bullied me and cast longing glances at the sacks of gold I had accumulated. Uncle Naboth, who, by the way, labored doggedly day after day, as he was commanded, often warned me against Larkin, but I had no fears, being assured the Major would protect me from the villain's hatred.

One or two others—Hayes and Judson, for instance —were evidently disreputable characters, and affected the society of Larkin when they were not at work. But in the main the miners were decent enough fellows, and seemed to have no thought above securing a fortune from the wealth of the golden sands. They paid me liberally, were just in their dealings, and labored industriously day by day so as to lessen the time of their captivity upon the island.

In the evenings the officers and crew of the "Flipper" were wont to gather in my hut, where they smoked their pipes and conversed more or less gloomily together. None of them, however, was greatly distressed at his fate, and it was wonderful how cheerful Uncle Naboth remained through it all. His silent merriment and sly winks were by no means lacking in these days of tribulations and hard work, and he found many opportunities to exercise his keen sense of humor. In one way his fortunes were really prospering, and each evening he weighed out the day's receipts, in golden grains, and calculated the profits to us on the sales. I suppose these must have been satisfactory, for he never complained.

I always slept in my hut, surrounded by the store of merchandise and my sacks of gold; but the rest of the crew of the ship had huts of their own, Nux and Bryonia occupying one together.

One night, after I had been asleep for some hours, I was suddenly awakened by the muzzle of a pistol pressed close to my forehead. I opened my eyes, and saw Larkin standing beside me. A tallow candle had been lighted in the hut, and I could see his evil features distinctly.

"Now, my lad," said he, "keep quiet an' you won't get hurt. But if you raise any rumpus or make a sound, I'll blow your brains out."

So I lay quiet but I kept my eyes open and eagerly watched what was taking place in the room. Besides

Larkin, there were present Daggett, Judson and Hayes —the worst characters in the camp. While Larkin remained beside me to threaten me with his pistol, the others spread out a blanket and dumped into it every sack of gold I possessed. This they secured by tying the corners of the blanket together. Next they spread another blanket and threw into it a quantity of canned meats and other provisions, afterwards tying them up as they had the gold. Then Hayes took the pistol and stood guard over me while the others crept from the hut. They were back in a few minutes, however, bearing another blanket heavily loaded. And now Larkin resumed his place beside me and the others caught up the three parcels and after extinguishing the candle slipped out of the doorway. There was a moon outside, I knew, but it was quite dark in the hut, and the consciousness of being at the mercy of the scoundrel beside me sent cold shivers creeping up my spine.

After waiting a few moments in silence Larkin spoke.

"Look a-here, Sam," he said gruffly, but in a low voice, "we've took some gold and other stuff, as ye know; but we ain't goin' to do murder unless we has to. If you've got sense enough to keep still for a solid hour, an' make no fuss, you'll live to get as much gold, or more, as we've just grabbed. But if you try to raise the camp, or foller us, I'll kill you before you know it. Now, I'm goin' to stand outside the door for a solid hour—you lay still an' count sixty seconds to a minute an' sixty minutes to an hour. If you move before that, you're a dead one; after the hour ye can howl all ye please, and the louder the better. I ought to stick a knife into you now; but I guess I'll wait outside the door, an' see if you mind what I tell you."

Then with a threatening flourish of his pistol, he slunk away, and as soon as he was outside the door I rose up and followed.

I knew he was lying, well enough, and that his threats were merely meant to terrify me into keeping silent until he escaped. He considered me a mere boy, and believed I would be too frightened to cause him any trouble.

But where could he and his fellow thieves go? How could they penetrate the wild thicket? That was the question that puzzled me. And then I remembered that Daggett was with them, who was reputed to be able to travel at will throughout the interior of the island.

When I reached the door and looked around I could at first see no signs of the man who had just left me. Then I discovered a dark form creeping along the edge of the jungle, and at once I sprang into the shade myself and crept after him. He was going slowly, and in my eagerness I closed up most of the distance between us, until I was dangerously near. But he did not look around, and while my eyes were fastened upon him he dropped to his knees, pushed aside a thick bush, and disappeared into the thicket.

That was all the information I wanted, just then; so I hastily marked the place by heaping a mound of sand before the bush, and then ran back to my hut as fast as I could go. I was terribly humiliated at being robbed so coolly of the gold that had been placed in my care, and rashly resolved that I would recover it by my own efforts, without disturbing the slumbers of my uncle or the Major. So, entering the hut, I secured three revolvers, of the Colt type, and several boxes of cartridges for them, all of which I had secretly smuggled from the ship and hidden among the groceries, for the Major had forbidden any of our crew having fire-arms. I had thought that an emergency might arise, some time, when these revolvers would be useful to us, and now I blessed my foresight in secreting them.

Having secured the weapons I ran quickly to the hut of Nux and Bryonia, and cautiously awakened them. At my first touch Bry sprang into the air and alighted on his feet.

"What's matter, Mars Sam?" he demanded.

"I've been robbed, Bry!" I panted.

"Robbed!" echoed Nux, who was now beside us.

"Yes; Larkin and his gang have taken every bag of our dust."

Through the dim light I could see their white eyeballs glaring at me in amazement.

"What you goin' do, Mars Sam?" asked Bry.

"I'm going to give chase, and make the rascals give it back. That is, if you will be my friends, and stand by me," I said. "By daybreak every bag must be in my hut again."

"Sure 'nough," murmured Nux.

"We ready, Mars Sam," announced Bry, quickly.

"Then take these revolvers, and follow me."

I gave a weapon to each, having hastily loaded them; and then I turned away, followed by the dark forms of the two Sulus.

"They're thieves, you know; burglars and outlaws," I said. "So if we have to shoot them down, no one can blame us."

They made no answer to this remark, and soon we had left the camp behind and reached the bush underneath which Larkin had disappeared. In a low voice I related what I had seen, and Bryonia, who was a master of woodcraft, at once dropped to his knees and vanished into the thicket. I followed closely after him, and Nux brought up the rear. After creeping a few paces through the underbrush Bry grasped my hand and raised me to my feet, and I discovered that we were now in a well-defined but narrow path which allowed us to stand upright.

It was dark as pitch in the grim forest, and we could only feel our way along; but it was not possible for us to get off the path, which had doubtless been cut by Daggett to afford his entrance into the interior of the island, and if our progress was slow those whom we pursued could not proceed at much greater speed themselves; so we crept along, stumbling over roots and tearing our clothes by brushing against the briars on either side, for a period of nearly an hour. Bryonia glided before us as stealthily as a panther, and often I was not certain but that he had left us far behind; but Nux made as much noise as I did, and puffed much harder to get his breath, so I did not fear being abandoned in the black wilderness.

The ground seemed to rise gradually as we penetrated into the wild interior, but the path remained as narrow as at first. Now that my first excitement and indignation had cooled, this midnight pursuit began to look doubtful of result. The robbers knew the way much better than we did, and they were so far ahead of us that we heard no sound of any sort to guide us. More than once I was tempted to abandon the chase, for my folly in undertaking it grew more and more evident; but the two blacks had no thought of turning back, and I was ashamed to call a halt.

Suddenly I ran plump into Bryonia, who grasped my arm as firmly as if it were in a vice, and held me rigid. Nux immediately ran into me, but stopped short at the moment of contact.

"What is it, Bry?" I asked, in a whisper.

"Look!" he answered, and swung me around in front of him. Then, as I peered into the darkness, a faint ray of light became visible. In a moment I perceived that it was growing bigger and brighter, and then I knew what it meant.

"They've gone into camp, and lit a fire!" said I, pleased to have overtaken them.

"Dey do'n' know we's coming," chuckled Nux, from behind.

But Bry stood like a statue, holding fast to my shoulders and peering over my head at the enemy. We could now see that the forest was much thinner here than at the point we had entered, and just beyond, in a little hollow where Larkin and his men were encamped, the trees grew quite scattered.

"Our best plan," said I, after a moment's thought, "will be to creep up to them and make a sudden attack."

"One, two, free, fou'," counted Bry, in his deep voice. "No use to 'tack, Mars Sam. Dey got guns, an' kill us all quick."

"We have our revolvers," I suggested, rather disappointed at his prediction.

"Nux an' I *might* hit somefin', an' we might not," said Bry. "If we hit somefin' it might be a man, an' it might not."

This was discouraging, and it called to mind the fact that I was not much used to fire-arms myself.

"Still, I don't mean to go back without doing something to recover our gold," said I.

"Wait!" whispered the black, and swung me around back of him again. How he managed this I do not know, for the path was very narrow. Next moment he disappeared, as if the earth had swallowed him up.

Nux gave a laugh, and sat down upon the ground. After a few moments I followed suit, squatting in the place I had been standing, for even from that distance I could see by the flickering firelight the dim forms of the robbers gathered around it.

And now I perceived that Bry's decision was wise. We were too far from camp to expect assistance in case of an emergency, even if our friends succeeded in finding the entrance to the jungle that was so cleverly concealed under the bush. So whatever was to be done must be done by ourselves—a boy and two black men against four desperate and well-armed villains, who would stop at no crime to retain the gold they had stolen.

Evidently they did not fear pursuit now, for we could hear the murmur of their voices as they laughed and shouted at one another.

We waited in silence for a long time, and as the gloom of the silent forest became intensified by the distant light I began to feel for the first time a thrill that was akin to fear.

Finally I noticed a black body wriggling its way toward us through the brush like some huge snake, and a moment later Bryonia stood before me.

"I creep close an' hear what dey say, Mars Sam," he reported. "Dey goin' watch all night. I watch, too. Tomorrow maybe we catch 'em. You an' Nux go sleep."

I protested at once that I was not sleepy; but Bry led us away from the path to a quiet place where he had found a bank of moss, and here he cautioned us to remain quietly. He himself crept once again toward the camp fire, and a moment later was wholly invisible. Nux whispered to me tales of Bryonia's skill as a woodsman, wherein it seemed he had excelled in his native land; but they grew monotonous, in time, and before I knew it I had fallen fast asleep on the mossy bank.

CHAPTER X.
THE ROCKING STONE.

When I opened my eyes it was broad daylight, and at first I could not remember where I was. But as I sat up I saw before me Nux and Bryonia, seated calmly side by side, with the wilderness all around me and the distant voices of the robbers echoing faintly in my ears. The sun was up, for I could see it glinting through the trees; so, as a recollection of my surroundings came back to me, I asked Bry what was going on.

He said the men were breaking camp, having slept late, and that presently they were going to travel still further into the interior. I could not imagine what they had in view, or where they expected to hide from the vengeance of the men they had plundered; but Bry declared we could follow them without ourselves being seen, so I decided not to give up until we had tracked them to their hiding place—if, indeed, they had one.

Presently we could see them tramping away to the southward, carrying the gold and provisions they had tied up in the blankets. There must have been two or three hundredweight of the gold, so the packages were heavy, and they had to take turns carrying them. But men seldom feel overburdened by the weight of gold, so we heard no complaints from the bearers.

Bry went on alone, hiding behind rocks and trees but keeping the men well in sight. After him trailed Nux, keeping Bry in sight; and then, as far away as I dared, I followed Nux, trying to imitate the example of the blacks and to hide myself as well as possible.

Before noon I grew hungry, for we had brought no provisions of any sort with us. The robbers paused to lunch, and then went on; but although I searched carefully, I could not find a morsel of food that they had cast aside. Of water there was plenty, for we crossed several small streams; but food began to be more precious than gold to me, and I vaguely wondered if I should die of starvation before I got back to camp.

At evening the men made camp again, this time in a little clearing strewn with fallen logs; and when Bry rejoined me in a clump of trees where Nux and I had halted, I told him frankly that I was faint with hunger, and that unless I could find something to eat I could not go on. I have no doubt the blacks were hungry, too; but they were more inured to hardship, and could bear it better.

But Bry volunteered to try to secure some food, and as soon as darkness had fallen he crept toward the camp, managing to approach to within five yards of the camp fire, around which the robbers sat smoking and talking. He was concealed by a huge log, behind which he hid, listening carefully to the conversation, which he afterward retailed to me.

"So far," Larkin was saying, "we couldn't have done better. By this time I guess we're pretty safe from pursuit."

"No one could find their way here in a year," boasted Daggett, his lean face grinning with delight.

"I'm the only man on the island as knows the trails."

"Are you sure you can lead us to that queer rock you tell of?" asked Judson, a little uneasily.

"Sure. And once there, we could defy an army," returned Daggett. "Then we can make our raft, row out to where the ship is, and sail away home."

Larkin gave a rude laugh, ending it with an oath.

"There'll be some tall cussin' in the camp," he said.

"Major'll be crazy," assented Daggett.

"I swiped every grain o' gold he had, while he lay a-snorin'," chuckled Hayes, a big ruffian who was called "Dandy Pete," in derision, because he was so rough and unkempt. "Pity we couldn't 'a' got all there was in camp."

"There's enough to make us all rich, my boys, anyhow," remarked Larkin. "It's nearly broke my back, luggin' of it, an' there's only four of us to divide."

At this they seemed to grow thoughtful, and all sat silently smoking for several minutes.

"What bothers me," said Judson, breaking the silence, "is how we're to get that blasted ship into some civilized port. There ain't a man here as knows anything about sailin'."

"That's all right," said Larkin, confidently. "The sun rises in the east, don't it? Well, all we've got to do is h'ist the sails and let the wind blow us towards the east. Some time or other we'll get to the American continent, and then we can run down the coast to

'Frisco. It's no trouble to sail a ship."

"We've got to get away, somehow," grumbled Judson, "or our gold won't be of any use to us. When are we going to divide?"

"When we get on the ship," said Daggett, promptly.

"When we're at sea will be better," added Larkin.

They looked at one another suspiciously.

"It's got to be a fair divvy," said Dandy Pete, with an oath, "or else there won't be so many to divide up with."

"What do you mean by that?" demanded Larkin, angrily.

"I mean I'll stick a knife in your ribs, if you try any trickery with me," replied Pete, scowling. "You made the terms yourself, and you've got to live up to 'em. It's a quarter each, all around."

"That's wrong!" yelled Daggett, springing to his feet. "I'm to have a third, for guiding you. If it hadn't been for me, you couldn't get away with the gold at all."

"Who promised you a third?" asked Hayes.

"Larkin."

"Well, let Larkin make it up to you, out of his own share. I'm going to have a quarter."

"And so am I," said Judson, fingering his revolver.

Larkin glared at them with a white face.

"We won't quarrel about it, boys," he said, after a time. "There's plenty for all, and we must hang together till we're out of danger. I'll take what you think is right, for my share."

"I'll take my third, an' no less," growled Daggett.

No one looked at him. Each seemed to be busy with his own thoughts.

Bryonia had chosen this especial log to hide behind, because the robbers had placed their sack of provisions upon it. While listening to the conversation I have recorded, the black had stealthily reached up his hand and managed to extract from the bundle a tin of corned beef and a handful of ship's biscuits. Then he wriggled carefully away, and in a few minutes had rejoined Nux and me, where we hid among the trees.

I think no food has ever tasted quite so delicious to me as did that tinned beef and stale biscuit. When divided amongst three there was little enough in each share, but it sufficed to allay our hunger and give us fresh strength and courage.

After we had eaten, Bry decided to go back again for more, since another opportunity to purloin from the bundle of provisions might not be offered us.

As it was very dark by this time, Nux and I crept nearer, to where a big rock lay; and here, hidden by the deep shadows, we were able to distinguish clearly all that transpired around the camp fire.

Bry being between us and the light, we could follow his creeping form with our eyes until we saw him lying safely hidden behind the log, with the bundle of food just over him. By this time all the robbers had lain down to sleep except Larkin, who had taken the watch and sat moodily smoking beside the fire, on which he tossed now and then a handful of fuel.

Suddenly, as he looked toward the sack that rested upon the log, he saw it move. In an instant a pistol shot rang out, and the robbers sprang to their feet with cries of alarm.

"Somebody's behind that log!" shouted Larkin, who was himself trembling with fear.

At once Bryonia arose to his feet, stepped over the log, and calmly advanced into the light of the fire, holding out his hand in greeting and smiling broadly into the angry faces confronting him.

"Don' shoot poor Bry," he said, pleadingly. "I'se run 'way to j'ine you."

"Run away!" exclaimed Larkin, while the others looked at the black suspiciously. "Why did you do that?"

"So's I won' haf to work any mo'," answered Bry. "Dey's jest killin' me in dat camp, luggin' bags o' sand an' washin' gold all day."

"Who came with you?" asked Daggett.

"Nobody 't all," declared Bry. "I seen yo' all leave de camp, an' so I crep' along after yo'. Wouldn't have let yo' know I was here, sure 'nough, but I got so hungry. I couldn't stand it no longer, so I tried to steal somefin' to eat, an' Mars Larkin he shot de gun at me."

"How did you know we had quit the camp for good?" enquired Pete, in a surly tone.

"Saw you take de gold, suh. So I 'pects you ain't comin' back agin', an' thought I'd j'ine yo'. If you'll take me 'long an' feed me, Mars Hayes, I'll help tote de gold."

Bryonia's statement was so simple that the miners were inclined to believe him. Nux and I, who had crawled nearer to the fire when the pistol shot rang out, could hear distinctly every word, and for a moment I was horrified that Bry should prove false and desert to the enemy. But Nux was chuckling gleefully, and whispered: "Dat Bry, he mighty clever boy, Mars Sam!" So I began to comprehend that Bry was acting a part, with the idea of saving Nux and me from discovery and ultimately recovering the gold. Therefore I kept silent and listened eagerly.

Evidently the miners were not of one opinion concerning the new arrival.

"Let's kill the nigger," said Daggett. "Then we won't run any chances."

"Don't be a fool," retorted Larkin. "Bry can be useful to us. He's the cook of the 'Flipper', I'm told, and besides helping to carry the gold, he can cook our meals when we get to sea, and help sail the ship."

"If he's run away from camp, why, he's one of us," said Judson, yawning and sitting down again. "And if it comes to a fight, he counts for one more on our side."

"But he don't get any gold," added Dandy Pete.

"Not an ounce!" declared Daggett.

"Don't want any gold," said Bry, composedly. "Only want to get away."

"All right," decided Larkin. "You can come along. But you've got to obey orders, and the first time I catch you at any tricks, I'll put a bullet into you."

Bry grinned from ear to ear, as if he considered this a good joke, and then he warmed his hands over the fire while Judson brought him something to eat from the bundle.

Afterward all lay down to sleep again except Larkin, who resumed his watch. It was too soon to put any trust in Bry, so the black, having eaten his fill, lay down beside the others.

Nux and I cautiously retreated to the rock, and consulted as to what we should do under these circumstances. The black man had perfect confidence in his comrade, and proposed that we should still follow the band of robbers and wait for Bry to find a way to communicate with us and assist us. This seemed reasonable to me, also.

As we were chilled to the bones in the cold night air, Nux suggested that we go into camp until morning, and led me a long distance back into the woods, where we finally came to a deep hollow. Here there would be little danger that a fire could be seen by the robbers; so we gathered together some twigs, and as I had matches in my pocket a fire was soon started that proved very grateful to us both. We then agreed to take turns watching until daylight, and while Nux lay down to sleep I took the first watch. But in some way—perhaps because the fire was so cosy and agreeable,—I gradually lost consciousness, and when morning came both Nux and I awoke with a start to find the fire out and the sun glinting brightly through the trees.

We made all haste toward the camp of the robbers, but when we arrived at the place we found it deserted. They could not have been gone long, however, for the embers of the fire were still aglow; and Nux, who was keen as a bloodhound on a trail, declared he would have no trouble in following the band.

Before we left, however, we made a search for food, and to our joy discovered behind the log a can of beans and some more biscuits, which Bry had evidently found an opportunity to hide there for our benefit. We began the chase even while we ate, for Nux picked out the trail with ease and threaded his way between the trees with absolute confidence.

It was nearly noon when he halted suddenly.

We had come to the edge of the forest. Before us lay a broad table-land, barren of any trees or brush whatever, and beyond this strip of rock the blue sea stretched away to the horizon.

"Why, we've crossed the island!" I exclaimed.

"Only one end of de island," corrected Nux. "De bay where our ship lays ain't half a mile away."

It surprised me that the shrewd black should know this, but I did not question his statement. Just now my attention was drawn to the robbers, who had halted upon the further edge of the table-land, which even from where we stood, could be seen to form a high bluff above the ocean. At this place it ran out into a little point, and just beyond this point, but separated from the mainland by a wide gulf, stood an island-like peak of rock, its flat surface on a level with the bluff. It must at one time have formed a part of the mainland, but some convulsion of nature had broken it away, and now a deep fissure isolated it from the bluff.

Nature was responsible for two other curious freaks. One was a group of tall pines, three in number, which grew on the separate peak where there seemed scarcely enough soil covering the rock to hold the roots of the trees. Yet on the main bluff there were no trees at all.

The other phenomenon was a great rock, that must have weighed thousands of tons, which lay upon the edge of the bluff so nicely balanced that it almost seemed as if a good push would precipitate it into the gulf below. It was triangular in shape, and the base rested on the bluff while its outer point projected far over the gulf till it towered almost above the isolated point of rock I have described.

The robbers, when we first saw them, were engaged in earnest consultation. It appeared that Daggett was explaining something about the great rock, for he pointed toward it several times, and then at the islet. The others leaned over the edge of the gulf, looked into the chasm below, at the triangular rock, at the barren islet, and then drew back and shook their heads.

Then Daggett, whom I had always considered a coward, did what struck me as being a very brave act. He climbed upon the sloping rock, and gradually crept upward on his hands and knees. When he reached a

110

point above the center the huge rock began to tremble. Daggett crept a little further along, and now the entire mass of rock, which was poised to a nicety, raised its vast bulk and tipped slowly outward. Daggett slid forward; the point of rock under him touched the islet and came to rest, and then he leaped off and stood safely upon the peak, while the rocking-stone, relieved of his weight, slowly returned to its former position.

A cheer went up from the men, and they hesitated no longer. Bry crept up the stone next, and was tipped gracefully upon the islet. One after another Hayes, Judson and Larkin mounted the rocking-stone and were deposited upon the rocky point, together with their bundles of gold and provisions.

We could not see very well what became of them, after this, for the big rock hid them from our view; but as it was evident they could not get back again—at least by the same means they had employed to reach the islet,—Nux and I made bold to creep out of our shelter and approach the point that jutted outward into the sea.

Then, to our surprise, we saw that the flat top of the rock was deserted. The robbers, together with Bry and the treasure, seemed to have vanished into thin air!

CHAPTER XI.
THE CAVERN.

From our better position we could now see the sides of the great rock which reared itself nearly a hundred feet from the shore and stood like some gigantic, flat topped obelisk, keeping guard by the lonely sea. Some ancient convulsion of nature, such as an earthquake or a lightning bolt, had evidently split it from the main precipice of rock near which it stood; for the huge crevice that separated it, and which extended entirely down to the beach, almost followed its outlines in every particular. But what had cast up that great rocking-stone, and placed it in so finely balanced a position that it could be made a curious but effective bridge to the isolated peak? No one can tell. Another freak of nature, doubtless, for no mortal hands could ever have moved so great a weight of solid rock.

And now was solved the problem of the mysterious disappearance of the robbers; for, looking over the edge, we saw them creeping slowly down the side of the cliff. A natural ledge, varying from one to three feet in breadth, led from the top down to the bottom, circling entirely around the crag with a sort of corkscrew regularity. It was a dizzy path, most certainly, and I did not wonder to see the men cling fast to the inner side of the rock as they crept down the tortuous ledge; but Daggett, who evidently knew the place well, led them fearlessly, and the others followed, dragging their burdens and the sacks of gold dust as best they could. I certainly expected to see one or more of them tumble headlong at any moment; but no accident happened and presently, as they descended, the path wound around the opposite side of the rock, and they were lost to view.

I wondered if I would see them again, and if it were wise to stick to my exposed post of observation; but while I pondered the matter Daggett came into view again, having passed around the rock. He was now two thirds of the way to the sands, and as he followed the ledge on the inner side, that lay next the face of the main cliff, I saw him suddenly pause upon a broader part of the path than the rest, and then disappear into the rock itself—or so it seemed to my gaze from where I watched. One by one the men came after him, and one by one the rock swallowed them up with their burdens; and now passed a period of tedious waiting.

Both Nux and I had counted the fugitives and saw that all had safely descended to this point, including Bry. But what had become of them now was a mystery.

"What shall we do, Nux?" I asked in indecision. "There's nothing more to be seen from here."

The black, whose eyes held a startled expression, made no reply; but he crept with me to a nearer and better position at the edge of the cliff beside the rocking-stone, and together we peered over into the abyss. Now, indeed, the strange disappearance of the robbers was explained, for from our present point of vantage we could see a black spot far down on the inner face of the column of rock, where the ledge passed, and this spot was evidently a cavity into which the men had penetrated.

"All we can do now," I said, with a sigh of regret, "is to wait until they come out. It would be foolish to follow them into that place."

Nux nodded an emphatic approval, and we proceeded to lie down upon our faces, so that our eyes just projected over the edge of the cliff, and in this position we watched as patiently as we could for something to happen.

It was fully an hour before the men reappeared. A distant sound of voices, raised high in angry dispute, was the first token that the desperadoes were quitting the interior of the rock. Then Larkin and Daggett came out and stood upon the ledge; the others crowding behind them on the narrow footing, while their guide pointed along the ledge that still continued to lead downward.

They were without burdens now, either of provisions or gold dust; but the two axes were carried over Bry's shoulder, and another man bore a coil of rope.

They seemed to be disputing together about something, and a few of the words reached our ears. Daggett was urging them to follow a plan he had proposed, while some of the others demurred.

"It's too hot to work," we heard one of the men declare.

"It's not too hot to hang," shouted Daggett, in reply, "and you'll hang, every mother's son of you, if we don't get to the ship!"

That seemed to be an effective argument, for after a

few more words of protest the men followed Daggett along the ledge, Bry coming last of all.

The path was broader from there on, and they made rapid progress, soon being again lost to our view around the rock. Just as Bry disappeared he looked up and saw Nux and me eagerly watching from above. For an instant he paused to wave his hand and grin at us reassuringly; then he passed around the edge and vanished after the others.

"Dat Bry don' 'pear to be much scared," said Nux, in an encouraged tone.

"No," I answered, thoughtfully. "He's got some plan in his head, I'm sure, to help us. But where have the men gone now?"

Nux could not answer this problem, but after a few moments it solved itself, for the robbers and Bry appeared upon the sandy shore, close to the water, and walked briskly along the narrow strip of beach between the lapping waves and the grim precipice of the mainland. It was not long before a bend in the coast hid them completely, and then we sat up and looked at one another inquiringly.

"What we do now?" asked the black.

"Let's go down the rock," I suggested, assuming to be braver than I really was. "They've left the gold behind them, that's sure; and the gold is what we're after, Nux. Once we have recovered that, it doesn't matter so much what becomes of the thieves."

"Won' dey come back?" enquired Nux, hesitatingly.

"I hope not," said I, truthfully. "At least not until after we've got back the gold. But there's no time to lose. Follow me."

Having thus assumed the leadership, I strove to banish all unmanly fear and boldly sprang on to the end of the rocking-stone that rested on the mainland. Slowly and with caution I crept up its incline until I was directly over the gulf. It was now that the stone should tip, but it seemed that my weight, being less than that of any of the men who had passed over, was not sufficient to balance the rock, so it began to look like a risky thing for me to climb further up the tapering point.

"But it's got to be done," I muttered to myself, setting my teeth firmly together; and then, summoning what courage I possessed, I lay close to the rock and crawled steadily upward, digging my toes desperately into the irregular hollows of the surface, to keep from sliding into the gulf that yawned below. Higher and higher I climbed, and at last the huge rock trembled and then gently sank beneath me. For a moment I was exultant; but I had crept so near to the slippery point of the wedge that I could find no rough projection to grasp with my fingers, and therefore as soon as my head became lower than my feet I slid headforemost to the point and tumbled off before the rocking-stone had reached a point of rest upon the peak.

Fortunately, however, I had been carried over the gulf, and although I lay, half-stunned, upon the very edge of the great precipice, I was not much hurt. In another moment I managed to drag myself to a position of greater safety, while the rocking-stone,

116

relieved of my weight, reared its nearest point into the air again and fell slowly back into its original position.

Nux, who had watched breathlessly my adventure and hair-breadth escape, was trembling violently when he in turn mounted the stone. But I called out to reassure him, and his greater weight caused the wedge to tip more quickly, so that he effected the passage to the rocky peak with comparative ease.

Once beside me the faithful fellow began rubbing my limbs briskly to renew their circulation and ease the bruises, and it was not long before I felt sufficiently restored to announce my resolve to continue the adventure.

"Come on, Nux," said I, scrambling to my feet, "we must get that gold before Daggett and his gang come back."

The black was staring at the rocking-stone, now removed from our table-like refuge by a good twenty feet.

"How we get back again?" he asked, in perplexity.

"I don't know," said I. "That's a question we'll have to face afterward. The main thing is to get the gold, and it's certain that if we can find no way to escape the robbers will be as badly off themselves."

Nux shook his head.

"Dat won' help us, Mars Sam," he said, gravely.

But already I was engaged in eagerly peering over the edge of the peak to find the ledge by which the men had descended, and in an instant I discovered it. It started with a projection scarcely six inches wide, which lay nearly four feet from the top, and it is small wonder that I looked at it dubiously, at first. For if I let myself over, and missed my footing, I would be tumbled sheer down the face of the cliff.

"I go first," decided Nux, who had also glanced over the cliff.

There was a crack in the rock, near the edge, which afforded him a hold for his hands, and clutching this the black let his body slide over until his feet touched the projection.

"Now, Mars Sam," he said. "You hold on me, an' come down."

This I quickly did, and found the feat much less difficult than I had feared. Just at the top where my companion's feet rested, there was sufficient incline to enable me to lean against the rock, and a few steps further on the ledge widened until the path was quite easy to follow.

I went first, followed closely by the black, and although it was not a descent one would have chosen for a pleasure excursion there was little of danger to be encountered by those with cool heads and determined hearts, such as we strove to maintain.

Round and round the great pillar of rock we crept, nearing the foot gradually until we came at last to the side facing the main cliff and found the opening of a large cavern beside us.

Filled with eager curiosity I took a step or two

inside, and found the cavern to be fully ten feet in height and about fifteen feet in depth. There was no light except that which came through the round entrance, and as this faced the side of the cliff it was so shadowed that it required a few moments for me to accustom my eyes to the gloom, so that I could see plainly the interior of the cave.

Its floor was strewn deeply with sand, an evidence that when the waves rolled high they rebounded from the face of the cliff and deposited their sand in the cavern. The marks of numerous footprints, however, were all that could be seen in the cave, and it did not take me a moment to guess what had occupied the robbers so long.

"They've buried the sacks of gold and the provisions under the sand!" I exclaimed.

"Sure 'nough," agreed Nux.

"It will take us some time to dig for them, for we don't know exactly where to look," I continued, reflectively, "so our best plan will be to go down to the beach and discover what has become of Daggett and his crew, and whether they're liable to come back here before night."

The black readily agreed to this, so we at once left the cave and continued along the ledge until we reached the sand.

The path became quite broad in this part, and our descent was therefore concluded very rapidly.

Once on the shore we walked briskly along until we had turned the bend in the beach, which curved to follow the lines of a little bay. Here we paused, for a long stretch of the beach was now opened to our gaze.

From this point the shore widened out, for the precipitous mainland shrank backward and decreased gradually in height until, a half mile or so further on, it reached the level plain and merged into a deep forest which grew almost down to the edge of the sea.

No human being was in sight, so we naturally concluded that the robbers had entered the forest.

Being curious to discover what they were doing, without hesitation we decided to follow them, and their path was easily traced by the footprints in the sand. These led straight to the forest, and although somewhat fearful that the enemy would discover our presence, we proceeded to walk boldly around the shore of the little bay until we came to the edge of the trees.

A sound of voices, mingled with the strokes of the axes, now guided us, and stealthily creeping among the thick underbrush we soon discovered the robbers busily at work.

Judson and Dandy Pete were trimming the branches from a fallen tree-trunk, while the others were rolling and dragging another big log toward the sea, the glistening waters being perceptible but a few yards away. Evidently the men were intending to build a raft, and after listening for a few minutes to their disjointed conversation we learned that the raft was designed to convey them and their stolen wealth to the ship.

While Daggett, Larkin and Bry tugged and dragged

at the log, Nux and I crept away to the shore, where we found two big logs already lying upon the sands. Also we could now plainly see, sheltered in another bay, the "Flipper" lying quietly at her anchorage, as Nux had wisely predicted.

The schemes of the robbers were now fully explained. Under cover of the forest by day, and hidden in their cave by night, they intended to complete the raft, and when it was ready it would not be difficult to steal away to the ship with the treasure, under cover of darkness, hoist the sails, and creep out to sea, bidding defiance to the Major and his comrades and leaving the miners and the "Flipper's" crew to perish on the lonely island.

But the construction of the raft would require time —several days, at least—for after getting the logs to the shore they must be fastened together by cross-strips secured with wooden pegs, since there was not enough rope in their possession to bind the tree-trunks together.

Once more returning to a part of the underbrush near which the men were employed, Nux and I settled ourselves to listen attentively to their conversation.

Presently we heard Daggett say:

"This rate we'll have the raft ready by Saturday, and Saturday night we'll take the ship."

"It's beastly hard work!" growled Dandy Pete, brushing with his sleeve the sweat from his brow.

"Yes; but it means liberty and riches to every one of us," said Daggett, and that was an argument none

121

cared to deny.

Just then I was startled at hearing low voices just beside me and instinctively I touched the black's shoulder and we crouched lower in the bushes. Nux, indeed, with a woodsman's instinct, was quite flat upon the ground, lifeless and invisible, and I strove to imitate him.

"It's as easy as can be," said the voice, which I recognized as that of Larkin. "We'll let the fools work until the raft is finished, and then we'll put our knives in their hearts, and have the gold for ourselves."

"How about Bry?" asked Judson, hoarsely whispering to his murderous comrade.

"Oh, he won't interfere any," was the reply. "And we need the nigger to help us work the ship."

"Can three of us manage the vessel?"

"Of course, with good weather. We'll have to take our chances of a storm, but the fewer there are to divide up, the bigger our fortunes will be. We won't give the nigger a cent, but go halves on the whole thing. Perhaps we can sell the ship, too, for a good sum."

"All right; I'm with you!" declared Judson, with an oath; and then the two conspirators crept away and rejoined the others, unconscious that their diabolical plot had been overheard.

CHAPTER XII.
WE RECOVER THE GOLD.

Thinking over the matter, I decided to return at once to the cave. The thieves would doubtless be occupied in the forest until sundown, and such a chance as this to secure possession of the gold might never occur again. For if Daggett or his men chanced to see our footprints in the sand, or suspected they were being spied upon, they would be liable to leave a guard in the cave thereafter.

So we softly crept from the forest and made our way back by the same route we had come, taking care to tread in the trail made by the robbers, so that our footprints could be less easily distinguished. We did not feel entirely safe from observation until we had regained the column of rock which towered into the air beside the precipitous cliff; but once our feet were on the narrow ledge both I and my faithful Sulu breathed easier, and with more deliberation accomplished the ascent to the cave.

"Now," said I, "we must work carefully, so that no spot of sand can escape us; for the thieves have taken care to disturb the surface everywhere, in order to throw any chance visitor to this hiding-place off the track. But we know the gold is buried in this cave, Nux, so it ought not to be a very hard job to find it."

Nux nodded, with his usual complaisance.

"We begin in back," he suggested, "and work front."

This seemed sensible, so I followed the black to the far end of the cavern, and falling upon our knees we immediately began digging with our hands into the soft sand.

For nearly an hour we steadily worked, finding nothing at all. Then, as I stopped to rest, I cast a careless glance along the rocky sides of the cave and thought that I saw a white mark upon the wall, a few feet toward the front. Springing to my feet I approached this point and discovered that a small cross had been made with a piece of chalk or a bit of white limestone.

"Here we are, Nux!" I cried, joyfully and at once began digging in the sand beneath the mark. A few minutes work proved that my sudden suspicion was correct; for Nux, who had straightway joined me, dragged one of the sacks to light, while I discovered another just beside it.

It was part of the stolen gold, sure enough, and my heart beat fast with excitement as I realized that the precious hoard was once more in my possession.

Only a part had been hidden in this place, we found; but now we had an unmistakeable clew to guide us, so that we had little difficulty in finding a second secret mark that resulted in the discovery of the balance of the treasure, as well as the sacks of provisions.

When all had been unearthed Nux asked:

"What we do now, Mars Sam?"

"Why, carry it away, of course," I answered, joyous and elate.

"Where?" enquired the black, simply.

I looked at him in surprise, and then realizing the meaning of the question, grew thoughtful again.

"You're right, Nux," said I. "It's going to be a harder task than I thought. We can't pass by the forest with it, that's certain; for Daggett and his followers would be sure to see us. On the other side, the cliff rises straight out of the sea, and there's no way to escape around it. All we can do, then, is to carry the gold to the top of this rock."

"Hm!" granted the Sulu. "Dat no good, Mars Sam."

"Why not?"

"No way to get off top of rock."

"True; but we can hide there, 'till the thieves go away to the ship. It isn't likely they'll climb up there again, for this cave is a better place to sleep in."

Nux seemed unconvinced, and I had none too much confidence in my own assertion.

"Tonight," said the black, in a dismal tone, "dey hunt for de gold. All gone. Robber very mad. Dey look ev'rywhere; den dey find us on rock. Den dey kill us."

"That's a pretty tough prophecy, Nux," I returned, as cheerfully as I could. "And it sounds likely enough, I confess. We've got the gold again, to be sure; but the robbers have got us; so we're worse off than we were before."

Nux took a lump of bread from a provision sack and begun to munch it leisurely. Noticing the action, and remembering that I also was hungry, I proceeded to follow the black's example.

While we ate, however, my Sulu was busily thinking, and so was I. As a result I presently gave my leg a delighted slap and began to laugh.

Nux looked at me with a grin of sympathy upon his black features.

"What's matter, Mars Sam?"

"Nux," said I, checking my amusement and trying to look grave and impressive, "there's an old saying that 'there's never a lock so strong but there's a key to fit it'. In other words, while there's life there's hope; never give up the ship; every sky has a silver lining!"

Nux looked puzzled.

"That's a lovely pair of trousers you're wearing, Nux," I continued, in a jocular strain. "They're made of the stoutest cloth Uncle Naboth could find in San Francisco, and I gave them to you out of the ship's stores only three or four days ago, because your old ones were so ragged."

Nux glanced at his wide-legged blue trousers and nodded.

"Now, old man," said I, "you've often told me you used to go bare-legged and bare-backed in your own island, so I'm going to ask you to go bare-legged a little while now, and lend me those trousers."

"Wha' for, Mars Sam?"

"To put the gold grains in, of course. The robbers

may look for the sacks of gold, when they come back, but they're pretty sure not to open them. Therefore, my friend we'll fix it so that they'll think their gold is all safe."

"How, Mars Sam?"

"By filling the sacks with sand, and burying them again where we found them."

Nux looked at me admiringly, and grinned until his mouth stretched from ear to ear and displayed every one of his white teeth.

"Good, Mars Sam!" he cried, and at once stripped the trousers from his legs.

I now hunted in the pockets of my jacket and brought out several small bits of cord, which I knotted firmly together. Then I tied the legs of Nux's trousers tightly at the bottoms, thus transforming them into a double sack of great capacity.

It did not take us long to transfer the gold dust from the canvas bags to the trouser-legs, and as soon as this task was accomplished we refilled the bags with sand and tied up as before. I was obliged to tear away a part of my own shirt to get material with which to tie the upper part of the trousers, for I did not wish to deprive poor Nux of his entire apparel. The Sulu looked funny enough, dressed only in his shoes and shirt, with his black legs between them, and more than once I was obliged to pause and laugh heartily at my comrade's appearance. But Nux didn't seem to mind, and soon the seriousness of our position and the necessity to hasten caused me to forget the queer costume of my follower.

We abstracted but a slender supply of provisions from the sacks, for we did not wish to arouse suspicion by taking too much. The next task was to bury the sacks of sand and the provisions exactly as they had been before, and to smooth over the surface of the sand and trample it down just as we had found it when we first entered the cave.

This being accomplished to our complete satisfaction, Nux lifted the heavy gold over his shoulder, one leg hanging behind his back and one in front, and started to mount the narrow ledge of rock with his burden, while I followed close behind to render any assistance I could.

The Sulu was a wonderfully strong man; but his task was a difficult one; although I tried to relieve him in the worst places by lifting a part of the heavy load.

Our progress was slow, for poor Nux had to stop frequently to put down his load and rest, and it was while we were on the outer surface of the rock, which faced the sea, that we were suddenly startled by hearing sounds that assured us the robbers were returning from the forest. Much time had been consumed in the cave, searching for the treasure and securing it, and now I began to fear we had delayed too long.

A hazardous climb.

Just at this time the men could not see us; but as soon as they mounted the ledge and began to wind around the tower of rock, they would be sure to catch sight of our forms, and then our fate would be sealed.

"Nux," I whispered, "pick up the gold and be ready to start. As soon as the thieves get back to the ledge we must go on, and keep the rock always between us and them, or we shall be lost."

Nux nodded, and obeyed without a word. It was often hard to tell, by the sound of their voices, just how far up the ledge the men had progressed; but fortune favored us, and only once did we lag behind enough for the first of the robber band to espy us. But that first person, by good luck, proved to be Bryonia, and the clever black at once pretended to stumble and fall, and so held the men that followed him in check until Nux and I had escaped around the crag.

Soon after this the robbers reached the cave, which they entered, thus enabling us to reach the top of the crag at our leisure.

Nux was nearly spent when at last he threw the laden trousers upon the flat top and tried to draw his tired body after them; but I gave him a hearty boost from behind, and then scrambled to the top unaided, nerved by the excitement of the moment.

For several minutes neither of us spoke. The black man lay panting for breath, with the perspiration streaming from every pore of his body, and I, filled with gratitude at our escape and the successful accomplishment of our plan, sat beside my faithful friend and fanned him with my straw hat.

The sun was sinking fast, by this time, and the shadows of the three tall pine trees that grew upon this isolated peak fell upon the spot where we rested, and cooled our sun-parched bodies.

Although at times a rough laugh or a shouted curse reached our ears from the cavern below, there was no indication that Daggett or his band had yet made the discovery that the place had been visited in their absence, and the treasure for which they had risked so much abstracted from its sandy grave.

When twilight fell I arose and with some difficulty rolled the trousers to a place nearer the center of the rock, where there was a small natural hollow; and then Nux and I sat beside it and ate again sparingly of the food we had brought.

It was while we were thus occupied that an incident occurred that filled us with sudden panic. For before our faces a man's head appeared above the edge of rock, and two dark eyes glared fixedly into our own.

At the moment I almost screamed with fright, so unnerved had my recent adventures rendered me; but Nux laid his broad hand across my mouth and arrested the outcry.

"It's Bry," he whispered, and even as he spoke the newcomer drew himself over the edge and crept on all fours to our side. I had no trouble in recognizing the friendly features then.

"Oh, Bry!" I said—softly, so as not to be heard by the robbers below—and clasped the black hands fervently in both my own.

Bry squatted beside us, his kindly face wreathed in smiles.

"Dey send me up here to see if anyone 'round," he whispered. "In a minute I go back and say 'no.'"

"Can't you stay with us, Bry?" I asked, pleadingly.

"Not yet, Mars Sam. Dey very bad mans, down dere. Dey kill you quick if dey find you."

"We've got the gold, Bry!"

"I know. I see you in de wood; I follow your footprints all way home; I see you climbin' up rock. Den I see de sand been dig up, so I knew you got gold."

"Did they suspect us at all, Bry?"

"No, Mars Sam. Dey too busy tryin' to kill each other. All want to have gold for himself, so all try to kill everyone else. Very bad mans, Mars Sam."

"They're going to take you on the ship, and make you sail it," said I.

Bry laughed, silently.

"I stay with them now, so they not find you," he said. "But when right time come I steal away an' come back to you. Did you fill sack with sand, Mars Sam?" glancing enquiringly at the stuffed trousers.

"Yes."

"That good," said Bry, approvingly. "They dig up one, when they come back, to see if all safe. Then they hide it again. Very good way to fool bad mans."

"But we can't leave here until they go away," I

remarked.

"No. Must be careful. Tomorrow they finish raft. Tomorrow night they go to ship. You stay here and hide till then. After de bad mans go, I come back to you, and we go to camp again."

"All right, Bry," said I, as cheerfully as possible.

Then the black bade us good-bye and returned to the cave to report to Daggett that no one was to be seen anywhere about. And now Nux and I, wearied by the adventures of the day, but buoyed by the hope that we might finally escape with the recovered gold, lay down upon the rocky eminence and, bathed by the moon's silver rays, slept peacefully until morning.

CHAPTER XIII.
THE CATASTROPHE.

I was awakened by the voices of the robbers, who were leaving the cave early in order to complete their raft by nightfall. It was evident that they had not suspected our intrusion into their retreat, or the fact that their stolen treasure had been taken from them. Indeed, they seemed in high spirits, especially Larkin and Judson, who were doubtless eager to carry out their nefarious plan of murdering their comrades as soon as the work on the raft was finished. Daggett might also harbor a conspiracy to secure the bulk of the treasure and probably all the members of the evil band were looking forward to this coming night to end their suspense and give them an advantage one over the other. "Honor among thieves" has often been quoted; but in this instance, as in many others that could be mentioned, the thieves were as lacking in honor as they were in honesty.

From my elevated perch I watched them file along the ledge to the sands, and upon reaching the level set off toward the forest. Not till they were well out of sight did Nux or I venture to rise upright and stretch our limbs.

The morning was warm and sultry. The sun gleamed hot in a cloudless sky and not a breath of air stirred the leaves of the three tall trees that stood at the edge of our towering rock.

"It's going to be a roasting day," I said to Nux, "and

135

we won't get any shade from those trees until afternoon. Do you suppose we dare go down to the cave for a while."

Nux shook his head.

"We all safe now, Mars Sam," he replied. "Better not run no risk wid dis yeah gold dust."

Thoughtfully I gazed toward the forest.

"Those fellows will be cool and comfortable enough in the shade," I remarked, rebelliously, "and I don't believe they'll come back through the hot sun until it's time to get the treasure. Let's go down to the sea and take a swim."

Nux was unable to resist the temptation; so, leaving the trousers full of golden grains resting on top of the rock, we made our way cautiously along the narrow, winding ledge until we reached the shore.

There was not a ripple on the sea. It lay as still and inert as a sheet of glass; but the water was cool, nevertheless, when compared with the stifling atmosphere, and so I and my black companion paddled in it for more than an hour, feeling much refreshed by our luxurious bath.

Afterward we ate our simple breakfast and then climbed the ledge as far as the mouth of the cave, where we sat down in the shade. Even that slight exertion quite exhausted us.

"We will be sure to hear them if they should by chance return," said I, "and we'll certainly be roasted if we get on top of this rock, where the sun can strike us.

I believe it's the hottest day I ever knew."

Meantime the men in the forest were finding their work far from pleasant, as Bryonia afterward told us. They were shaded from the sun, it is true; but the air they breathed was as hot as if it came fresh from an oven, and the least exertion caused the perspiration to stream from their pores. So there was considerable grumbling among them and a general shirking of work that made their progress slow. Even Bryonia, who was fairly heat-proof, found he had little energy to swing his axe, although he made a pretense of working as industriously as ever.

"Never mind, boys," said Daggett, when noon had arrived and they were eating the luncheon they had brought in their pockets. "The raft will be big enough to carry us and the gold to the ship, I'm sure, for the sea is as still as a mill-pond. We'll just get these two logs to the shore, and fasten them to the others, and call the thing a go. What do you say?"

They agreed with him readily enough. As a matter of fact the raft might suffice to carry them all, but none of them believed that all five would embark upon it, so many murderous schemes were lurking in their minds.

Wearily they dragged the two logs toward the sea, but much time was consumed in this operation, and the day was far spent before the raft was complete and ready to launch.

Most of the men had stripped themselves naked, to work more comfortably, for the heat was well-nigh unbearable; but now, as they stood ready to push the raft into the water, the sun suddenly disappeared and a cold chill swept over them.

"We're going to have a storm," cried Daggett, looking curiously into the sky. "Better leave the raft where it is, my lads, and make for the cave."

The warning was unquestionable. Already a low, moaning sound came to their ears across the sea, and the sky grew darker each moment.

With one accord the men seized their clothing in their arms and ran along the beach toward the cave, while tiny points of lightning darted here and there about them, casting weird if momentary gleams upon their naked forms.

Nux and I sitting half asleep by the mouth of the cave, were warned by the first chill blast that swept over us that the weather had changed and a storm was imminent. Springing to my feet I looked fearfully at the darkening sky.

"What'll we do, Nux?" I asked. "This will bring our enemies back here in double-quick time."

"Better climb on top de rock, Mars Sam," advised the Sulu.

"But it'll rain—floods and torrents, probably—and thunder and lightning besides."

"'Spect it will, Mars Sam. But rain wont hurt us much."

"And Daggett's gang will, if they catch us. I guess you're right, Nux. Come along."

As we started along the ledge the wind came upon

us in sudden gusts, and the sky grew so dark that we almost had to feel our way. It was necessary to exercise great care, both to find a secure footing and to cling fast to the face of the rock, to prevent our being blown into the abyss below; but we struggled manfully on, and presently reached the top, where Nux hoisted me over the edge and then scrambled after me.

By this time the lightning was playing all around us, and we were obliged to crawl carefully on hands and knees to the little hollow in the center of the rock, where we were to an extent shielded from the fierce gusts of wind. Even then I feared we would be blown away; but Nux shouted in my ear to hold fast to the gold, which served as a sort of anchor, and enabled us both, as we lay flat in the hollow, to maintain our positions securely.

And now the lightning began to be accompanied by sharp peals of thunder, while the wind suddenly subsided to give place to wild floods of rain. At intervals could be heard the shouts of the robbers, who had reached the rocks and were creeping along the ledge to their cave. All the elements seemed engaged in a confused turmoil, until I was nearly deafened by the uproar. I tried to ask a question of Nux, but could not hear my own voice, and gave up the attempt. The thought crossed my mind that we had been very foolish to climb to this peak of rock, where we were exposed to the full fury of the storm, and I wondered vaguely, as I clung to the sack of gold we had risked so much to secure, how long it would be before the wind swept us away, or we would be annihilated by a bolt of lightning.

Presently an arm was laid across my back, as if to

protect me, and raising my head I saw by the light of a vivid flash that Bryonia had joined us and was lying in the hollow at my side.

I wondered how the daring Sulu had ever managed to reach us; but the strong arm gave me a new sense of security, and impulsively I seized the black man's hand and pressed it to express my gratitude and welcome.

An instant later a terrible crash sounded in my ears, while at the same time a blast of fire swept over the rock and seemed to bathe our three prostrate figures in its withering flame. Again came a crash; and another — and still another, while the crisp lightning darted through the air and made each nerve of our bodies tingle as if pricked by myriads of needle points.

Half bewildered, I raised my head, and saw the great rocking-stone sway from side to side and then plunge headlong into the gulf that lay between the precipice and the solitary rock whereon we reclined. And I felt the mighty column of rock shake and lean outward, as if about to topple into the sea, while the impact of the fallen mass reverberated above the shriek of the wind and the thunder's loudest roar.

Instinctively I braced myself for the end—the seemingly inevitable outcome of this terrible catastrophe; but to my surprise no violent calamity overwhelmed us. Instead, the lightning, as if satisfied with its work of destruction, gradually abated. The blinding flashes no longer pained my closed eyes with their vivid recurrence, and even the wind and rain moderated and grew less violent.

CHAPTER XIV.
BURIED ALIVE.

Terrified beyond measure by the awfulness of the storm, I gave little heed to the fact that the rocky hollow in which I lay with the two faithful blacks had filled with water, so that our bodies were nearly covered by the pool that had formed. My head still rested on the trousers packed with gold, and one arm was closely clasped around a leg containing the treasured metal grains. So I lay, half dazed and scarcely daring to move, while the rain pattered down upon us and the storm sobbed itself out by degrees.

I must have lost consciousness, after a time, for my first distinct recollection is of Bryonia drawing my body from the pool to lay it on a dryer portion of the rock, where the overhanging trees slightly sheltered me. The sky had grown lighter by now, and while black streaks of cloud still drifted swiftly across the face of the moon, there were times when the great disc was clear, and shed its light brilliantly over the bleak and desolate landscape.

Within an hour the rain had ceased altogether, and stars came out to join the moon; but still we lay motionless atop the peak of rock, worn out by our struggles with the elements and fitfully dozing in spite of the horrors we had passed through.

Bry was first to arouse, and found the sun shining overhead. There was no wind and the temperature of the morning air was warm and genial. The black's legs pained him, for in his terrible climb up the rock during the storm a jagged piece of rock had cut his thigh and torn the flesh badly. He had not noticed it until now, but after examining the wound he bathed it in the water of the pool and bound it up with a rag torn from his shirt.

While he was thus occupied Nux sat up and watched him, yawning. They spoke together in low tones, using the expressive Sulu language, and had soon acquainted each other with the events that had occurred since they separated. Their murmured words aroused me to a realization of the present, and having partially collected my thoughts I began to rub my eyes and look wonderingly around me.

The top of the rock was no longer flat, but inclined toward the sea. The three tall trees also inclined that way, instead of growing upright, and the neighboring cliff of the mainland seemed further removed from us than before. Something appeared to be missing in the landscape, and then I suddenly remembered how the rocking-stone had leaped into the gulf during the storm.

"All safe?" I asked, looking at my black friends gratefully.

"All safe," answered Bry, smiling.

"It was a dreadful night," I continued, with a shudder. "Have you heard anything from the robbers yet?"

"No, Mars Sam."

"They're probably sleeping late. Anyhow, they can't

have gone away on the raft yet."

Bry shook his head.

"All very wicked mans, Mars Sam," he said. "Even in big storm, while we climb up to cave, Mars Daggett tell me to go behind Pete an' push him off rock."

"The villain!" I exclaimed, indignantly.

"He tell me if I not push Pete off, he kill me," continued Bry, with a grin.

"What did you do?"

"When they run into cave, I run by it, an' come here. That's all, Mars Sam."

"You did well, Bry. If they climb up here after you, we'll fight them to the death."

"No climb rock any more, Mars Sam," said Bry, soberly.

"Why not?"

"See how rock tip? Only fly can climb rock now."

"I believe you're right, Bry!" I cried, startled at this dreadful assertion; "and, if so, we're prisoners here. Let us see what it looks like."

I crawled rather stiffly down the inclined surface to the edge overlooking the sea, and one glance showed me that it would now be impossible for anyone to walk along the narrow ledge.

While I looked a sharp cry of horror from Nux

reached my ears, and swiftly turning I hastened with Bry toward the place where the black was leaning over the gulf that separated the peak from the mainland.

"What is it, Nux?" I asked, anxiously.

But the Sulu only stood motionless, pointing with one finger into the abyss, while his eyes stared downward with an expression of abject fear.

We both followed his gaze, and one glance was sufficient to fully acquaint us with the awful catastrophe the vengeance of the storm had wrought.

The huge rocking-stone, weighing thousands of tons, which for ages had remained delicately balanced upon the edge of the chasm, had been struck by a bolt of lightning and torn from its base. Crashing into the gulf, a point of the great, wedge-shaped boulder had entered the mouth of the cave where the desperadoes sought shelter, and, crowded forward by its own weight, it had sealed up the robbers in a living grave, from whence no power of man could ever rescue them.

It was this mighty wedge, crowded into the space between the slender peak and the main cliff, that had caused the former to lean outward; and in one comprehensive look we were able to read the whole story of the night's tragedy—a tragedy we had instinctively felt in the crash of the storm, but could only realize now.

"Poor fellows!" I whispered, softly, forgetting in my awe that they had been our relentless enemies. "It was a terrible fate. Perhaps they're even now sitting in that dark hole, shut off from all the world and waiting for death to overtake them. Isn't it dreadful."

The blacks glanced at one another without reply; but I noticed that they exchanged a secret sign which their pagan priests had taught them when they were boys, and which was supposed to propitiate the demon of retribution. To their simple minds Daggett and his gang of cut-throats had been properly punished for their wickedness.

But for my part I am glad to remember that at the moment I ignored the fact that these men were wicked, and grieved that four human beings had suddenly been cut off in the prime of their manhood. The recollection of their crimes might temper my regret afterward, but just now my thoughts were all of sorrow and commiseration.

Nux roused me from my reflections by asking:

"What we do now, Mars Sam?"

"I don't know," I answered, despairingly. "If we can't escape from this rock we are little better off than those poor fellows below us. See! the stone, as it fell, tore away the ledge completely."

"No climb down, any way at all," said Bry, squatting upon the rock and clasping his knees with his hands.

"We haven't any rope, or enough clothing to make one," I continued, striving to be calm and to force myself to think clearly. "But if we remain up here it won't take us long to die of thirst or starvation. The aggravating thing about it is that the mainland is just too far away for us to leap across to it. We're in a bad fix, boys, and no mistake."

Bry gazed reflectively at the trees.

"If we had axe," said he, "we chop down tree, and make fall across the gulf."

"Ah! that's a clever idea," I cried; but my elation quickly subsided, and I added gloomily, in the next breath: "only we have no axe."

Bry made no answer, but sat thoughtfully gazing around him. Presently he began to creep around the table of rock on his hands and knees, examining every part of its surface with great care.

At one place, where the edge of the rock was jagged and of a harder character than the rest, he paused to make a more thorough examination, and then he drew out his one-bladed jack-knife and began prying into the rock with its point.

Nux and I immediately crept to his side to see what he was doing, and soon Bry had loosened a piece of rock that weighed about five pounds. It was flat on the lower surface and of irregular circular form. This fragment the Sulu examined with great care, and struck it sharply against the rock without breaking it. It seemed to meet his approval, for he laid it carefully aside and at once attempted to pry up another portion of the hard rock. Then, when he had again succeeded, he sat down and began cautiously chipping one piece of rock against the other, until he had brought the first fragment to a wedge shape that resembled a rude axe.

"Ah! I understand now what you're about, Bry," I

exclaimed, delightedly. "Do you think you can make it work?"

Bry nodded.

"That way we make axe in Jolo-Jolo," he said, proudly.

He now handed the rude implement to Nux, who seemed to comprehend without words what was required of him, for he at once began rubbing the edge of the stone axe upon a rough portion of rock to smooth and sharpen it more perfectly.

Meanwhile Bry pried up more rock and formed a second axe-head, and so for several hours the men labored patiently at their task, while I, unable to be of assistance, sat watching them with breathless interest.

When the second axe was ready for Nux to sharpen, Bry climbed up the trunk of one of the tall pines and, selecting a branch of the size he desired, with much effort cut it from the tree with his knife.

Then he descended, trimmed the branch, and, began fashioning it into an axe-handle. He made no attempt to render it graceful or beautiful, you may be sure. The one requirement was service, and the wood was tough and strong enough to answer the purpose required.

By the time the handle was ready Nux had worn the edge of the first rude stone axe to a fair degree of sharpness, and with it Bry split the end of the handle far enough down to wedge the axe-head between the pieces. Then he bound the top together with strips of bark cut from a young limb, which was far stronger than any cord would have been.

A clumsy instrument it seemed to be, when it was finished; but Bry balanced it gravely in his hands, and swung it around his head, and nodded his full approval and satisfaction.

"Now we chop down tree," he announced.

Of the three trees that fortunately grew upon the column of rock, two were evidently too short to reach across the gulf from where they stood. But the third was close to the edge, and towered well above its fellows; so this was the one Bry selected. A woodsman would probably have laughed at the strokes dealt by the Sulu; but Bry knew what he was about, for he had chopped trees in this way before. Too hard a blow would have crushed the stone edge of the weapon, and a prying motion would have broken it at once; so the black struck straight and true, and not with too much force, and slowly but surely wore through the stalwart trunk of the tree.

When the axe got dull he unbound the bark thongs and exchanged it for the other, while Nux re-sharpened it. This consumed a good deal of time, and the day was far advanced before Bry decided that the chopping was deep enough to allow them to fell the tree. This they did in a peculiar way, for Nux climbed into the high branches and then, aided by Bry and me, who pushed from below, he began swaying the tree back and forth, his own weight adding to the strain, until suddenly it gave way at the stump and—slowly at first, but with ever accelerating speed—fell with a crash across the gulf.

It looked like a trying and dangerous position for Nux; but the black cleverly kept on the outer side of the branches, which broke his fall so perfectly that even as the tree touched the cliff he sprang to the ground safe and uninjured.

"Hooray!" I shouted, in delight; for this bridge removed from my heart all terrors of starvation and imprisonment, affording us a means of leaving the islet of rock as soon as we pleased to go.

But the sun was even now sinking below the horizon; so we decided not to effect the crossing until morning. Nux climbed back over the swaying trunk, and after he had rejoined us we ate the last crumbs of food we possessed for our supper and then lay down to sleep.

Having passed the day in idleness I found I was not very tired or sleepy; but the blacks were thoroughly exhausted by their labors, and they welcomed the rest as only weary men can.

Long after they were snoring I sat in the moonlight thinking of our strange adventures of the past twenty-four hours; the recovery of the gold, the destruction of the robbers, and our present means of release from the dangerous pinnacle that had threatened to hold us fast prisoners. And I realized, with a grateful heart, that I owed all of my good fortune and narrow escapes to the faithful black men, and made a vow that I would never in the future forget the services they had rendered.

CHAPTER XV.
THE MAJOR GIVES CHASE.

Meantime there had been much excitement and confusion in the camp when it was discovered that several of the men, including Nux and Bry, and even "the boy Sam," had disappeared during the night with most of the gold dust that had been accumulated.

I can relate fairly well what occurred, for I heard the story often enough afterward.

The Major was furious with rage, at first, and sent at once for Uncle Naboth, whom he accused of being at the bottom of the plot to rob him.

Mr. Perkins was so full of his own anxieties that he paid little attention to the red-bearded giant's ravings.

"I'm afraid Sam's in trouble," he said, nervously.

"In trouble! You bet he is," yelled the Major, "I'll skin him alive when I catch him."

"That's the point," answered Uncle Naboth. "How are we to find him again? I'll risk your hurting the boy, if we can only find out where they've taken him."

"Your niggers are gone, too," the Major reminded him.

"That's the only thing that gives me hope, sir," retorted my Uncle. "Those black men are as faithful and honest as any men on earth, and I'm thinking they're gone after Sam to try to rescue him."

"Then you think he's been kidnapped, do you?"

"Of course. The men that are missing are the worst of your lot—the ones that have caused you the most trouble in every way. There's not a man from the 'Flipper's' crew among them. The way I figure it out is that Daggett, Larkin, Hayes and Judson have made a plot to steal all the gold, and escape with it. They robbed you first, and then they robbed Sam, and when the boy tried to make a fuss they just kidnapped him and took him along with them."

"How about the niggers?" asked the Major, sarcastically.

"That puzzles me, I'll admit," acknowledged my Uncle. "Bry and Nux may have seen the thieves get away with Sam, and followed after them, to try to rescue him. That's the only way I can figure it out just now. But we're losing time, Major. What's to be done?"

"Two things. Get back the gold, and shoot down the robbers like dogs. They can't get away, you know. They're somewhere on this Island, and I mean to find them."

"There's the ship."

"What of it?"

"If they get aboard and sail away we'll be in a bad box."

"How can they get aboard? We've got the small boats."

"They can make a raft, or even swim out to the ship," returned Uncle Naboth, shrewdly, "I tell you, Major, you're wasting time. Why don't you do something?"

The Major glanced at him as if undecided whether to be angry with him or not. But Mr. Perkins was undoubtedly right, and the miners were gathering outside the door with curses and threats against the men who had robbed them, for the news had quickly spread throughout the camp.

So their leader sent six men, heavily armed, in the ship's long-boat to board the "Flipper" and protect the vessel from being captured. These were all his own men, for he still suspected that the "Flipper's" crew were in some way implicated in the theft.

Then he picked four miners and four of the sailors to form a party to search for the robbers, and decided to lead the band himself and to take Uncle Naboth with him. The rest of the men were ordered to resume their work of washing out gold.

"I'm going to trust you, Perkins," said the Major, "for your loss is as great as ours, and you seem anxious over that boy of yours. But if I meet with any treachery I'll shoot you on the spot; and if I find that Sam Steele is one of the thieves I'll show him no mercy, I promise you."

"Quite satisfactory, sir," answered Uncle Naboth, calmly. "Only let us get started as soon as possible."

It was a puzzle at first to know in which direction to look for the fugitives; but Ned Britton had been carefully inspecting the edge of the forest, and came upon one of the paths Daggett had made in the course of his various wanderings inland. It was not the one we had taken, but away they started through the thicket, on a false scent, and the entire day was consumed in a vain search.

As they sat over their camp fire at evening Ned proposed that they try the other side of the island the following day.

"It's there where the ship lies anchored, sir," he told the Major; "and it's most likely the men are in that neighborhood. The paths we've been following today are old trails that lead nowhere in particular, and there's no use going any further in this direction."

This proposition was so sensible that the Major at once agreed to it, and daybreak saw them tramping through the tangled underbrush toward the opposite side of the Island. Britton, who had a good sense of direction and knew about where the ship lay, undertook to guide them, and was fortunate enough to strike the trail of the robbers about the middle of the afternoon. The tracks lay directly toward the beach, and they pressed on with renewed vigor; but the heat was terribly oppressive in the more open country they had now reached, and the men were all exhausted by the long tramp. When, a little later, the sky grew black and the storm burst upon them, they withdrew to a thick grove of trees and rigged up a temporary shelter with their blankets, beneath which they passed the night.

The storm raged all around them, and occasionally the crash of a fallen tree startled their nerves; but the high cliff broke the force of the wind and the lightning was less severe than it was directly on the coast.

Uncle Naboth thought of me more than once during this rage of the elements, and hoped I was safe from harm; indeed, his anxiety was so great that he scarcely closed his eyes throughout the night.

At daybreak they left their shelter and gazed wonderingly at the scene of devastation around them. The storm had wrought fearful havoc everywhere, and when they resumed their journey their progress was necessarily slow and difficult.

Still they labored on, and in the afternoon passed through the forest and came upon the coast directly opposite the place where the "Flipper" still rode at anchor under bare masts. She seemed to have escaped all danger from the storm, and although the sea was still rolling high the good ship nodded her prow to each wave with a grace that betokened she was still in good condition.

"Well, boys, the robbers haven't got her yet!" cried Uncle Naboth, delightedly.

"No; but they've had a try for it already," said the Major, significantly, as he pointed to a half-finished raft that had been lifted high by the waves of the previous night and wedged fast between two great trees. "Evidently the scoundrels don't know we have sent a squad to guard the ship."

"We're on their trail, all right," remarked Ned Britton, after examining the crudely constructed raft carefully. "But where do you suppose they are?"

"Somewhere on the coast, of course," said Uncle Naboth. "Let's walk up the edge of the bay to the inlet, and see if they're in that direction."

So they made for the inlet, failing, of course, to find any traces of the thieves. They were seen from the deck of the "Flipper" by the men who had been sent aboard in the long boat, and the Major signaled them to remain where they were for the present.

After a brief halt the little band retraced their steps to examine the coast in the other direction, and another night overtook them within hailing distance of the rocky peak where I and my two blacks were resting beside our newly acquired bridge to await impatiently the morning. But the Major's party was, of course, unaware of this, and went into camp in a hollow where the light of their fire was unobserved by us.

At daybreak, however, Uncle Naboth and Ned Britton were up and anxiously exploring the coast; and presently they saw, a little distance away, the tall form of Bryonia walking carefully across our tree trunk. The black almost fell into the arms of Uncle Naboth, as he stepped off the tree and the old man's first anxious question was:

"Where's Sam?"

"Here I am, Uncle!" I called from my rock. "I'll be with you in a minute, but we've got to get the gold over first."

"The gold!" cried Uncle Naboth, in amazement. "Have you got it, then, after all?"

"To be sure," said I, with a touch of pride, "every

grain of it!"

Uncle Naboth groaned.

"I didn't think as you'd do it, Sam, my boy," he said regretfully.

"I couldn't have done it, without Nux and Bry," I answered, not understanding that I had been accused of the theft.

The old man turned reproachfully to Bry, who stood grinning beside him.

"Did I ever teach you to steal, sir?" he demanded, sternly.

"Takin' gold from robbers ain't stealin'," replied the black, in a calm tone.

"What robbers?"

"Daggett, an' Pete, an'——"

"Oh, I see!" exclaimed Uncle Naboth, a light breaking in upon his confused mind. "They stole the gold from the camp, I suppose, and you and Sam have followed them up, and got it back again?"

"That's it, exactly, Uncle!" I declared from my side of the precipice, where I could hear every word spoken. "I'll tell you the whole story bye and bye."

Just then I was wondering if I dared cross the tree. It seemed very frail, and the rounded trunk was difficult to walk upon. Should I lose my balance there were only a few slender branches to cling to in order to keep from toppling over into the gulf below.

Bry saw my dilemma, however, and running lightly across the tree again he caught me up bodily and perched me upon his broad shoulders.

"Hold fast, Mars Sam," he called, and the next moment stepped out fearlessly and, while Uncle Naboth held his breath in grim suspense, the black crossed the swaying tree and dropped me safely on the other side.

The old man had barely time to grasp both my hands in a warm clasp when the big Major came up, blowing and sputtering, with the balance of the party.

"Well, where's the rest o' the thieves?" he cried out, glaring fiercely at me and then at Bry.

"Under that rock, sir," I answered gravely, with a shudder at the recollection of their dreadful punishment; and then, in as few words as possible, I told the story of our adventures, relating how we had followed the robbers and recovered the gold, and of the great storm that had sent the rocking-stone hurling into the chasm to seal up the evil band in a living tomb.

Even the Major was impressed by the weird tale, and Uncle Naboth wiped the sweat from his brow as he leaned over the cliff and marked the immense wedge of rock that had closed forever the mouth of the cavern.

"It seems there's no one left to punish," growled the red-beard, in a low voice; "and I'm glad the fate of those scoundrels was taken out of my hands. As for you, young man," turning suddenly to me, "you've acted splendidly, an' so have the niggers. Let's shake hands all 'round!"

I felt my face turn as red as the Major's whiskers at this unexpected praise.

"Hooray!" yelled Ned Britton, and the others joined him in a mighty shout of approval.

Then Ned and Bry crossed the tree to where Nux was still standing on the peak, and hoisted the loaded trousers to Bryonia's back. Nux crossed over in front and Ned Britton behind the bearer of the precious gold, to save him if he made a misstep; but their caution was unnecessary. The big Sulu was as sure-footed as a goat, and safely deposited his burden at the Major's feet. Then we all returned to the near-by camp for breakfast, after which, the gold being taken from the trousers and distributed into several small packages, that they might be more easily carried, Nux was given his leg-coverings again, to his infinite satisfaction.

"And now," said the Major, "we'll make tracks for the camp. We've been away a long time, but we've got the gold back, and got rid of the worst characters among the lot of us; so there's nothing much to

159

grumble over, after all."

CHAPTER XVI.
THE GRAVE CAPTAIN GAY.

Perhaps it was only natural that I should become the hero of the miners when the camp was at last reached and the men learned the strange story of our recovery of the gold. Nux and Bry also came in for a good share of praise, which they well deserved, and it seemed as if the adventure had established a permanent good feeling between the gold seekers and our crew of the "Flipper." There was no more suspicion on either side, and when the Major made a new division of the recovered gold he generously insisted that I should receive even more than I had been robbed of, for my share. Whatever the Major's faults might be, he was certainly liberal in his dealings with others, and Uncle Naboth was greatly pleased with the profitable result of an adventure that had at first threatened to ruin the fortunes of the firm of Perkins & Steele.

No one mourned very much over the death of the men who had stolen the gold; on the contrary, there was a feeling of general relief that the four desperadoes were unable to cause any more trouble. Therefore the camp resumed its former routine, and the miners set to work with renewed vigor to wash out the golden grains from the rich sands of the inlet.

It was about this time that the grave and reserved Captain Gay proved himself to be a genius, and by an act of real cleverness that crowned his name with glory materially shortened the stay of our entire community on the island.

The Captain had worked side by side with the common sailors, for the Major showed no favoritism, and insisted that every able-bodied man should perform his share of the work. Even Uncle Naboth had from the first day of our capture toiled from morning till night; but he accepted his tasks with rare good nature, and frequently confided to me, in his droll way, that his enforced labor had added ten years to his life.

"I was gettin' altogether too chunked and fat," he said one evening, "and likely enough I'd 'a' been troubled sooner or later with apoplexy or dropsical. But now I've lost twenty or thirty pounds weight, an' feel as lively as a cricket in a hornet's nest. Work's a good thing, Sam. I'm glad the Major made me do it. Probably he's saved my life by his cussedness."

Captain Gay had been working at the upper end of the inlet near to the place where a slender mountain stream fell from a precipice above and mingled its fresh water with that of the inlet. This stream fell upon a rocky bottom, but in course of years it had worn a bowl-shaped hollow in the rock, which could be distinctly observed through the transparent water.

"There ought to be a lot of gold in that hollow," Ned Britton had remarked to the Captain one day. "I've an idea all the gold we find in the sands of the inlet has been brought here by the mountain streams."

"I've been thinking that, myself," answered the Captain; but it was a week later that he climbed the rock and followed the bent of the stream for nearly a mile, marking carefully the lay of the land.

The next morning he went to the Major with his plan, which was nothing less than a proposal to turn the stream from its bed, several hundred yards above, and let it follow a new course and reach the inlet a hundred feet distant from its present fall.

The Major stared thoughtfully at the Captain for a time, and then followed him up the stream and made a careful examination of the territory. The result was an order for all the seamen of the "Flipper" to place themselves at the disposal of Captain Gay and obey his orders.

In three days they had built a dam of rocks and brushwood nearly across the stream, and pried away the banks in another place to allow the water to escape by the new channel.

The fourth day the opening was closed in the dam, and the stream plunged away on its new course, leaving its former bed practically dry.

Immediately the men ran down to the inlet, where the Major himself waded to the hollow caused by the previous fall of water and dipped a pan of sand from the cavity. Upon examination it proved richer in gold than any of us had anticipated, the sands containing many small nuggets which, being heavier than the grains of metal, had been accumulating for many years in the basin.

All hands were set to work in this locality, and inspired by the rich harvest that rewarded their toil, they labored early and late, until the bags of dust and nuggets had become so numerous that even the Major was filled with amazement.

But this was not all that was gained by turning the mountain stream from its bed. In several hollows up above Captain Gay discovered rich deposits of small nuggets that were secured with ease, and two weeks later the Major called a meeting of all the members of the party on the sands before his tent.

"Boys," said he, "we've got enough to make every one of us rich for life. What's the use of staying here longer? I'm getting homesick, for one, and a good many of you are longing to get back to the States and begin spending your piles. What do you say—shall we board the ship and go home?"

"Yes!" they yelled, without a dissenting voice.

"Then," said the Major, "tomorrow we'll divide the spoils, so that every man has his honest share; and then we'll pay our passage money to Mr. Perkins and sail away home."

The division was accomplished with very little dissatisfaction or friction, for the worst elements in our assorted company had been removed, and the Major was absolutely just in his decisions. One or two, to be sure, grumbled that the provisions from the "Flipper" had been purchased at too high a price, or that too much of the gold was set aside to pay for the passage back to San Francisco; but not one objected when the Major set aside three heavy bags of gold to reward Captain Gay for his clever feat in turning the mountain stream.

When Uncle Naboth and I, in the seclusion of my hut, had figured out our share of the profits, the old man was hugely delighted.

"My partner!" he exclaimed, slapping his thigh with enthusiasm, "it's paid us better than three trips to Alaska! We've nearly made our fortunes, Sam, my boy, and if we get safe home again we can thank the Major for making us his prisoners."

It did not take our party long to transfer all their possessions to the decks of the "Flipper," where the ship's carpenter and part of the crew had been sent beforehand to clear up the rigging, ship a new rudder, and make some repairs that had been rendered necessary by the storm that had driven us to this strange island.

To my own inexperienced eyes the damage had been so great that it seemed as if the sailors would require weeks in which to make the vessel fit to put to sea again; so that I was astonished, when I went aboard, to note how quickly the task had been accomplished. Indeed, the "Flipper" seemed as trim and staunch as when she last sailed out of the Golden Gate, and doubtless she was fully able to bear us all safely home again.

All our party having been put aboard, together with their property, Captain Gay ordered the anchors hoisted, and at eleven o'clock on the morning of September 16th, the "Flipper" headed out to sea before a fair breeze.

The quarters aft had been given up to the miners, most of whom were obliged to swing hammocks in the cabin. The mate offered his little room to the Major and bunked with the sailors in the forecastle; but Captain Gay and Mr. Perkins retained their own rooms, and so did I, in order to watch over the firm's gold, which was stowed carefully away in my lockers. You may be sure I was glad to get back to my books and my comfortable bed again, and overjoyed to find myself on the way to a more civilized land.

As the ship stood out to sea, the Major, who had been pacing the deck with a thoughtful brow, noticed Captain Gay taking his bearings with the aid of the sextant, while I stood by observing him. At once the big man's countenance cleared, and he strode over to us and anxiously watched the Captain while the latter made notes of his observations. Several of the miners likewise seemed interested, but it was evident they did not understand in the least what the Captain was doing.

No sooner, however, had Captain Gay returned to his cabin, where at his request I followed him, than the Major knocked for admittance, and being invited to enter he cautiously closed the door after him and said:

"You've relieved me of a great worry, Captain. I was afraid we'd never be able to find this island again. But the sextant gives you the latitude and longitude, doesn't it?"

Captain Gay nodded, and looked thoughtfully out of his little window at the fast receding island.

"That island's mine," continued the Major, in a stern voice; "and I shall claim it until some one else proves a better right to the place."

Still the Captain made no reply.

The Major stared at him as though he had just discovered the man.

"Does any one else aboard know how to use those instruments?" he finally asked.

"No one," answered the Captain, briefly.

"Then the secret is safe with us," resumed the Major. "I'll just trouble you, my good fellow, to give me the exact latitude and longitude of the island. I'll mark them down in my note-book."

"Come to me tomorrow noon," said Captain Gay.

"Why tomorrow noon?" with a sudden frown.

"Can't you understand? Don't you know it requires hours to figure out so complicated a problem?"

"Oh, does it?"

A nod.

"Well, I'll come in tomorrow. But understand, not a word of the true reckoning to a soul on board. Not even to Perkins or the boy here, who has no business to be listening to this conversation, and had better forget it. The island is mine!"

Captain Gay sat silent; merely drumming with his fingers on the little table before him. The Major gave him another curious look and stalked away, whistling softly to himself, as if something had occurred to puzzle him. Indeed, the Captain's face was so set and stern that it made me uncomfortable, and I soon left him and returned to my own room.

The "Flipper" made good time during the afternoon, and before darkness fell those on board saw the island where they had labored so hard and endured so much, gradually sink into the sea and disappear.

The breeze held all through the night, and daybreak found the sturdy ship plowing steadily onward over the waste of gray waters. The sailors had fallen into their usual routine and performed their labors with mechanical precision, while the miners lay around the deck and watched them with the interest landsmen usually show when on a sailing ship.

At the stroke of twelve I saw the Major promptly approach the Captain's room, where I knew the seaman was busily engaged in writing.

Wishing to learn the result of this second interview I crept forward and without hesitation established myself beside the door, which the red-beard had carelessly left ajar. I even ventured to peer curiously through the opening; but neither of the men observed my intrusion.

The Major for a moment stood staring with the same wondering gaze he had bestowed on Captain Gay the day before; but suddenly his face brightened and he said:

"By Jupiter! I've struck it at last!"

"Struck what?" asked the Captain, looking up.

"The resemblance that bothered me. You're the living image of that man Daggett, who caused us that trouble on the island. It's a wonder I never noticed it before."

The Captain flushed, but said nothing.

"No relation, I hope?" queried the Major, grinning.

"To Daggett?"

"Yes; the scoundrel who stole our gold."

Captain Gay had resumed his writing, but said, lightly, as if the matter was too preposterous to be treated seriously:

"Is it likely, sir?"

But already the Major's mind had turned to a more important subject.

"I've come for that little memorandum, sir."

"What memorandum?" asked the Captain, quietly.

"The location of the island."

"Oh; I can't give it to you," said the other. "When you left this room yesterday the draft from the open door caught the paper I had made my figures on, and carried it out of the window. So the record is lost."

"Leave this room, sir!"

"Lost!" The Major stared at him in amazement.

"Absolutely lost, sir."

"Do you mean to tell me you don't know where that island is?" demanded the Major, fiercely.

"I haven't the slightest idea of its location. During the night the helmsman altered our course several times, steering by the stars. I think we're going in the right direction, but I can tell better when I've taken our observations for today. Unfortunately, however, that won't help us to locate the island."

The Major sat down heavily on a chest. The information he had received fairly dazed him, but his gaze remained firmly fixed on the Captain's expressionless face.

After a time he gave a laugh, and said:

"I told you yesterday that island was mine. I'll take that back. It's *yours* and mine. You'll share it with me, Captain Gay, I'm sure."

"It is still yours, Major, as far as I'm concerned. If I knew its location, I would tell you willingly. But I don't. You'll have to find your property yourself."

The Major sprang up with an oath.

"You infernal scoundrel!" he cried, "do you think I'll be played with like this? Give me the location of that island, or by the nine great gods, I'll kill you where you sit!"

"Leave this room, sir."

The Captain was angry too, by this time. He stood erect and pointed with dignity to the doorway, from which I dodged with alacrity.

"I command this ship, sir," he said, "and here my will is law. I'll endure no browbeating, Major, or any insolence from you or any of my passengers. On the island I obeyed you. Here you will obey me, or I'll lock you fast in your cabin. Leave this room!"

The Major stood irresolute a moment. Then sullenly and slowly, he quit the cabin and returned to the deck.

Even to my wondering but immature intellect it was evident that Captain Gay had won the battle.

CHAPTER XVII.
WE GIVE UP THE SHIP.

The "Flipper" made good time, and sighted the Oregon coast on the morning of the fifth day. From there she followed the dim outlines of the distant land down to the Golden Gate, and cast anchor safely and without event in the bay of San Francisco.

The Major had been sullen and ill-tempered during the entire voyage, but although he made repeated efforts to see Captain Gay privately and renew his request for the location of the golden island, that officer positively refused to hold any further communication with him.

Therefore the Major was helpless. After all, the Captain might be speaking the entire truth; and if so all argument was useless. Threats do not affect a man of his temperament, and beyond threats the Major did not care to go, even to secure the information he wished. Bribery, in such a case, was absurd. Therefore nothing could be done but bear the disappointment with a good grace. The Major's fortune was, for the present, ample, and I wondered why he should ever care to visit the island again.

As soon as the anchors were dropped the miners clamored to be set ashore, and by night they had all quitted the ship and established themselves in lodgings in the town, from whence they at once flocked to the bankers and began to turn their golden grains into cash.

Uncle Naboth and I remained on board another day. There were settlements to be made with the sailors and various other details that needed attention at the close of the voyage; so that I was kept busy with my books of accounts and Uncle Naboth stood constantly at my elbow to give me the necessary instructions.

We both longed to be on shore again, however; so as soon as the last formalities were completed, we put our heavy sacks of gold into a boat and carried them to the docks, from whence an escort of our trusty sailors accompanied us to the bank wherein Mr. Perkins was accustomed to keep his deposits.

So many ships had lately returned from Alaska bearing gold from the mines that Mr. Perkins' heavy deposit aroused no wonder except as to its extent, and the banker warmly congratulated him upon his good fortune in making so successful a voyage.

Both Uncle Naboth and I remained at the bank until every sack of gold had been carefully weighed and sealed, and the proper receipt given. Then, breathing freely for the first time since the gold had been in our possession, we repaired to my Uncle's former lodging house, where Mr. Perkins was warmly welcomed.

"We'll have the best dinner tonight the establishment can set up, Sam, my boy," said the old man, rubbing his hands gleefully together; "for we've got to celebrate the success of the new partnership. You must 'a brought the firm luck, my lad, for this here is the biggest haul I've heard of since I've been in the business. We're rich, nevvy—rich as punkins!"

"How much do you suppose we're worth, Uncle?" I

enquired, rather curiously.

"I can't tell exactly, o' course, till after we've got the quality of our gold properly graded, and put it on the market; but my opinion is, we're at least fifty thousand dollars to the good."

"As much as that!" I exclaimed, greatly elated.

"Full as much, I judge."

"Then," said I, drawing a sigh of relief, "I can pay Mrs. Ranck that four hundred dollars I owe her for my board."

Uncle Naboth made a wry face.

"It's a shame to throw good money away on that old termagan'," he remarked, "and I've no doubt she's been overpaid already, by stealin' the contents o' Cap'n Steele's chest. But if it'd make you feel easier in your mind, Sam, I'll fix it so you can send her the money as soon as you like."

"Thank you, Uncle," I replied, gratefully, "I'll never be happy until the debt is off my shoulders. Whether she's entitled to the money or not, I promised Mrs. Ranck I'd pay the debt, and I want to keep my word."

"An' so you shall," said Uncle Naboth, with an approving nod.

We feasted royally at dinner, and afterward Uncle Naboth took me to the theatre, where we sat in the top gallery among the crowd of laborers and sailors, but enjoyed the play very much indeed.

"Some folks who had just banked fifty thousand,"

remarked my Uncle, reflectively, "would want to sit down there among them nabobs, in a seat that costs a dollar apiece—or perhaps two dollars, for all I know. But what's the use, Sam? Do they hear or see any better than we do up here?"

"Probably not," I answered, with a smile.

"Then we're getting as much fun for our quarter as they get for a dollar," declared Uncle Naboth, chuckling, "an' tomorrow mornin' we'll be so much richer, an' nothin' lost by it. Sam, the secret o' spendin' money ain't in puttin' on airs; it's in gettin' all the pleasure out of a nickel that the nickel will buy. 'Live high,' is my motto; but do it economical. That's the true philosophy o' life."

Next morning, as we were sitting in Uncle Naboth's little room, we were surprised by the entrance of Captain Gay. He was accompanied by two of the sailors from the "Flipper," bearing in their arms the easily recognized canvas sacks of gold from the island.

The Captain motioned his men to place the sacks upon the rickety table, (which nearly collapsed beneath the weight), and then ordered them to leave the room. When they were gone he carefully closed the door and turning to my Uncle said, abruptly:

"There, sir, is every grain of gold I got in that accursed island. The most of it was given me for turning the bed of the mountain stream, as you will remember."

"No more than you deserved, sir," said Uncle Naboth, puffing his pipe vigorously.

176

"It ought to be worth a good deal of money," continued the Captain, his voice faltering slightly.

"Twenty thousand at least, in my judgment," said Uncle Naboth, eyeing the sacks.

"Well, sir," announced Captain Gay, with decision, "I want to exchange this gold for a bill of sale of the ship."

"What! The 'Flipper?'"

"Yes, sir."

Uncle Naboth winked at me gravely, as if to convey the suggestion that the man had gone crazy.

"Cap'n," said he, after a pause, "I don't mean to say as Sam and I won't sell the ship, if you'd like to buy her; but the tub is old, and has seen her best days. She's worth about six thousand dollars, all told, and not a penny more."

"You must take all that gold or nothing, sir."

"What do you mean?" asked my Uncle, in amazement.

Captain Gay sat down and looked thoughtfully out of the window.

"Perhaps I must take you into my confidence," he remarked, in his slow, quiet tones, "although at first I had thought this action would be unnecessary. I've an idea I'd like to own a ship myself, and to trade in a small way between here and Portland."

"And the golden island, occasionally; eh, Cap'n?"

177

returned Uncle Naboth, shrewdly. "I've heard from Sam here how you lost the paper containing your observations; but, I suppose you could find the place again, if you wanted to."

Captain Gay flushed a deep red.

"Sir," he answered, "you wrong me with your suspicions. I shall never revisit that island under any circumstances. Nor do I wish anyone else to do so. That is the true explanation of why I lost that paper."

"Did you lose it?"

"I threw it overboard."

Uncle Naboth whistled.

"I'm free to confess, sir, that I'm all at sea," he said.

The Captain arose and paced the room with unusual agitation.

"Mr. Perkins," said he, "I once had an older brother, who, when a boy, robbed my father and ran away from home. I never saw him again until we reached that island, where I recognized my erring brother in the man who called himself Daggett."

Uncle Naboth scratched a match, and relit his pipe.

"I marked the resemblance between you," he observed, "but I thought nothing of it."

"To my grief I saw that he had not altered his course for the better," resumed the Captain. "Of his final theft of the gold and the awful judgment that overtook him and his fellows you are well aware. I shall never forget the horror of those days, sir. It seems to me that that isolated unknown island is my brother's tomb, where he must lie until the call of the last judgment. I do not wish anyone ever to visit the spot again, if I can help it."

"That's nonsense," declared Uncle Naboth, coldly.

"Perhaps so; but it's the way I feel. That's why I don't wish to touch the gold. I'll take the ship in exchange for it, but I won't use the stuff in any other way, or have anything more to do with it."

"You're foolish," said Uncle Naboth, with a sternness quite foreign to his nature. "But if you really want to give away a matter of twenty thousand for an old hulk that's worth about six, I'll let you have your way."

"That's my desire, sir," announced our visitor, meekly.

"Well, then, we'll go to a lawyer and draw up the papers. Sam, you stay here and look after the gold, till I get back."

"Very well, sir," I replied, full of wonder at this queer business transaction.

Together they left the room, and it was an hour before Mr. Perkins returned.

"I signed for both of us, partner," he said, briskly, "an' the 'Flipper's' now the sole property of Cap'n Gay. With the money this gold will bring, we can buy a ship twice as good as the old one, in which, with good luck to back us, we ought to make many a prosperous voyage."

"Why do you think he did it, sir," I enquired musingly.

"It's just one of two things," replied Mr. Perkins. "Either the man's a bit cracked, as I've sometimes suspected, and really feels sentimental about his brother's death, or else he's got a sly scheme to make trips to the island in an old ship that won't attract attention, and bring away many cargoes of gold. That ain't so unlikely, Sam. No one will remark on Cap'n Gay's owning the old ship he's commanded for years; but if he bought a new one, and started out for the island, he might be watched and his true business suspected. Either the feller's mighty deep, or mighty innocent; but it ain't our business to decide which. We've got the money, and now we'll look for a newer and finer ship."

"New England's the best place to buy a good ship, sir. I've often heard my father say so," I suggested.

"Then let's go to New England," returned Uncle Naboth, promptly. "We'll travel together, and you can run up to Batteraft and pay the old hag that money."

"I'd like to do that," said I, greatly pleased. "It would do me good to see her surprise when she finds I've earned so much money already."

"Then it's all settled," declared Uncle Naboth. "I'll go up to the village with you, and see fair play. 'Twould be a fine chance to give that cankered Venus a piece of my mind, just as a parting shot."

"Would you dare, sir," I asked, recollecting his

former experience with Mrs. Ranck.

"Would I dare? Do you take me for a coward, then?" demanded the old man, indignantly.

"No, sir, but I remember——"

"Never mind that, Sam. I was worried about other things that day, and wasn't quite myself. But *now*— well, just wait till I get the old serpent face to face. That's all!"

"All right, Uncle. When shall we go?"

"Just as soon as we've paid all the bills and settled our accounts for the last voyage. A week'll do that, I reckon. An' now, partner, just run out and hire a closed carriage, and we'll get Cap'n Gay's gold to the bank as soon as possible. Sam, my boy, if this streak o' luck holds good we'll be the envy of Rockyfeller in a few years!"

CHAPTER XVIII.
UNCLE NABOTH'S REVENGE.

Ten days later, having paid all our indebtedness and converted every ounce of our gold into ready money that was deposited to the credit of "Perkins & Steele," at the bank, we started on what Uncle Naboth called our "voyage" across the continent.

We had both taken a strong liking for Ned Britton, who has stood by us so faithfully at the island; so Mr. Perkins decided to make Ned the mate of the new ship, when she had been purchased. For this reason, and because the sailor wished to revisit some of his relatives in the East and make them happy by sharing with them his prize money, Ned also traveled on the same train with us.

"Britton's judgment will be useful in helping us to pick out a ship," said the old man. "I'm glad he's going with us."

Nux and Bryonia had promptly deserted the "Flipper" as soon as they found that Captain Gay had purchased her, and I think my hardest task was to leave the simple black men behind me. They declared that they belonged to "the firm" and must be given places on the new ship, and this both Uncle Naboth and I were anxious to do, as we knew we could never again find such loyal and unselfish servants. But it would be folly to take them east until all arrangements had been made. So I found them comfortable lodgings, and supplied them with all the money they could possibly require until they were sent for. At the last moment they were at the station to see the train move away, and were so fearful of the iron monster that was to carry their friends on the journey that they cautioned me again and again to be very careful in my actions.

"'Fore all, Mars Sam," said Nux, earnestly, "doan' you go skeer dat injine on no 'count. W'en it's skeert it smashes ev'ything into mush."

"'Pears gentle 'nouf now, Sam," added Bry; "but don' you trust it, no how. 'Tain't safe, like a great sail an' a stiff breeze."

"Right you are, lad," cried Uncle Naboth, approvingly. "Injines is an invention of the devil, Bry, but good Christians can use 'em if they only watch out. An' now, good bye, an' take care o' yourselves till we get back or send for you."

On account of our great wealth, Mr. Perkins had decided to take a tourist sleeping-car for the trip, rather than sit up in the seats of the common cars all night.

"Sleepin' cars is a genuine luxury, Sam," he said, "an' only fit for the very rich, who've got so much money they won't miss it, or the very poor, who've got so little there's no use savin' it. I guess we can afford the treat and the bunks in this 'ere tourist car is jest as big as the ones in the high-priced coaches ahead. So as soon as we get clear of 'Frisco, let's go to bed."

"But it isn't dark yet, Uncle," I protested. "It won't be bedtime for hours."

"Sam," replied the old man, earnestly, "do you mean to say you're goin' to pay for a bed and let it lay idle? That's what I call rank extravagance! I've seen it done, on my travels, o' course. I've known a man to pay three dollars for a bed, an' then set up half the night in the smokin' cars before he turns in. But do you s'pose the railroad company pays him back half the money? Never. They just laughs at him and keeps the whole three dollars! To pay for a thing, and use it, ain't extravagance; but to buy a bed, and then set up half the night is. Why, it's like payin' for a table-day-haughty dinner an' then skippin' half the courses! Would a sensible man do that?"

"Not if he's hungry, Uncle," said I, laughing at this philosophy.

"If he ain't hungry, he buys a sandwich, an' not a table-day-haughty," cried Uncle Naboth, triumphantly.

Nevertheless, being fully conscious of my newly acquired wealth, I recklessly sat up until bedtime, while my thrifty Uncle occupied his "bunk" and snored peacefully. The journey was accomplished in safety, and from Boston we took the little railway to the seaport town of Batteraft.

During the last hours of the trip Uncle Naboth had become very thoughtful, and I frequently noticed him making laborious memoranda with his pencil on the backs of envelopes and scraps of paper which he took from his wallet. Finally I asked:

"What are you writing, Uncle?"

"I'm jest jotting down the things I mean to say to

that old female shark at Batteraft," was the reply. "I tell you, Sam, she's goin' to have the talkin'-to of her life, when I get at her; and she'll deserve every word of it. I'll let you pay her first, so's the money account will be square; an' then I'll try to square the moral account."

"Will she let you?" I enquired doubtfully, for I had a vivid remembrance of Mrs. Ranck's dislike of any opposition.

"She can't help herself," replied Uncle Naboth, seriously. "If you knew the things she up an' said to me that day I tackled her before, Sam, an' the harsh an' impident tones she used to say 'em with, you'd realize how much my revenge means to me."

"Why didn't you resent it then, Uncle?"

"Why, she took me by surprise, an' I didn't have time to collect my parrergraphs, and that's the reason. Also it's the reason I'm figgerin' out my speeches aforehand this time, so's I won't be backwards when the time comes. You can't thrash the cantankerous old termagen' like you would a man, but you can lash her with speeches that cuts like a two-edged sword. At sarcasm and ironical I'm quite a professor, Sam; but them talents would be wasted on Mrs. Ranck. With her I'll open my vials o' wrath an' empty 'em to the dregs. I'll wither her with scorn, an'—an'—an' tell her just what I think o' her," he concluded, rather lamely.

I sighed, for the mention of Mrs. Ranck always recalled to me the fate of my poor father. The landscape began to grow very familiar now, and presently the train swung into the little station where I had so often stood in my younger days to watch the passengers get on and off the cars.

Ned Britton at once walked on to the tavern, but as the afternoon was only half gone Uncle Naboth and I decided to go on up to my father's old home without delay and have our carefully planned interview with Mrs. Ranck. The banknotes I was to pay to her lay crisply in my new pocket-book, and I was eager to be free of my debt to the cruel woman who had aspersed my dead father's character and driven me from my old home.

Uncle Naboth walked very fast at first, but while we ascended the little hill his pace grew gradually slower, and as we reached the well-remembered bench beneath the trees, from whence our first view of the cottage was obtained, my uncle suddenly set himself down and wiped the perspiration from his forehead with the well-remembered crimson handkerchief.

"We'll rest a minute, Sam, so's I can get my breath back," he gasped. "I'll need it all, presently, and hill-climbin' ain't my 'special accomplishment.'"

So I sat down beside him and waited patiently, eyeing the while rather sadly the old home where I had once been so happy.

It seemed not to have changed in any way since I left it. The blinds of my little room in the attic were closed, but those of the lower floor were thrown back, and a column of thin smoke ascended lazily from the chimney, showing that the place was still inhabited.

In spite of myself I shivered. The autumn air struck me as being chilly for the first time, and the declining sun moved slowly behind a cloud, throwing the same gloom over the landscape that was already in my heart.

"Are you ready, Uncle?" I asked, unable to bear the suspense longer.

"Jest a minute, Sam. Let's see; the opening shot was this way: There's folks, ma'am, that can be more heartless than the brute beasts, more slyer than a roarin' tiger, more fiercer than a yellow fox, an' —"

"That isn't right, Uncle Naboth," I interrupted. "The fox is sly and the tiger —"

"I know, I know. Them speeches is gettin' sorter mixed in my mind; but if that she-devil don't quail when she hears 'em, my name ain't Naboth Perkins! Perhaps I ought to have committed 'em more to memory — eh, Sam? What do you say to waitin' till tomorrow?"

"No, Uncle. Let's go to her now. You can reserve your vials of wrath, if you want to; but I shan't sleep a wink unless I pay Mrs. Ranck that money."

"All right," said the old man, with assumed cheerfulness. "There's no time like the present. 'Never put off 'til tomorrer,' you know. Come along, my lad!"

He sprang up and led the way with alacrity for a few steps, and then slackened his pace perceptibly.

"If I'm goin' to forget all them speeches," he whispered, in a voice that trembled slightly, "I might jest as well have saved my time a-composin' of 'em. Drat the old she-pirate! If she wasn't a woman, I'd pitch her into the sea."

By this time I was myself too much agitated to pay attention to my uncle's evident fright on the eve of battle. The house was very near now; a few steps further and we were standing upon the little porch.

"You knock, Uncle," I said, in a whisper.

Uncle Naboth glanced at me reproachfully, and then raised his knuckles. But before they touched the panel of the door he paused, drew out his handkerchief, and again wiped his brow.

I felt that my nerves would hear no further strain. With the desperation of despair or a sudden accession of courage—I never knew which—I rapped loudly upon the door.

A moment's profound silence was followed by a peculiar sound. Thump, thump, thump! echoed from the room inside, at regular intervals, and then the door was suddenly opened and a man with a wooden leg stood before us. He was clothed in sailor fashion and a bushy beard ornamented his round, frank face.

For an instant we three stood regarding one another in mute wonder. The open door disclosed the long living-room, at the back end of which Mrs. Ranck stood by the kitchen table with a plate in one hand and a towel in the other, motionless as a marble statue and with a look of terror fixed upon her white face.

Singularly enough, I was the first to recover from my surprise.

"Dad!" I cried, in a glad voice, and threw myself

joyfully into the sailor man's arms.

"Why—Cap'n Steele, sir—what does this mean?" faltered Uncle Naboth. "I thought you was dead an' gone long ago, an' safe in Davy Jones's locker!"

CHAPTER XIX.
THE CONQUEST OF MRS. RANCK.

I regret to say that my father's welcome was not especially cordial. Nevertheless, he was for some reason evidently pleased by the sudden appearance of his son and his brother-in-law. Releasing himself gently from my clinging embrace, he said, in his deep, grave voice:

"Come in and sit down. I never thought to see you again, Sam; and, much less you, Naboth Perkins. But now that you're here, we'll have a few mutual explanations."

Mrs. Ranck, a few paces behind him, was bristling like a frightened cat.

"If them thieves an' scoundrels enters this house, I'll go out!" she fairly screamed, in her shrill voice.

"Be quiet!" commanded the Captain, sternly. "This is my house; and, although it's all that my friends have left to me," he added, bitterly, "I'm still the master under my own roof. Sit down, Perkins, sit down, Sam, my lad."

A sudden tenderness that crept into the last words seemed to rouse the woman to fury.

"That's the boy that robbed you!" she cried, pointing at me a trembling, bony finger. "That's the boy that skinned the house of all your valeybles and treasures as soon as he thought you was dead, and

190

couldn't come back to punish him! An' stole all my savin's too; and swore he'd be a pirate and murder and steal all his life; an' that the man," turning fiercely upon my horrified uncle, "as aided an' abetted him in his wickedness, an' threatened to kill me if I interfered with Sam's carryin' away of your property! Cap'n Steele, how dare you harbor sich varmints? Drive 'em out, this instant, or I'll go myself. This house can't hold Sam Steele, the robber, and me at the same time!"

Captain Steele looked toward me gravely as I stood regarding the woman with unmistakable amazement. Then he turned to Naboth Perkins, to find the little man doubled up in his chair and shaking with silent laughter. A moment later he began to gasp and choke and cough, until, just as he appeared to be on the verge of convulsions, he suddenly straightened up and wiped the tears from his eyes.

"Cap'n Steele, sir," he said, "this is the best show I ever had a reserved seat at, an' the admission's free gratis for nothin'! Why, you measly old she-tiger," turning with stern abruptness to Mrs. Ranck, "did you ever think, fer a minute, that such a lyin' tale as you've trumped up would deceive grown men?"

Mrs. Ranck turned away and caught her shawl from a peg.

"I'll go," she said, sullenly.

"No, you don't!" exclaimed Mr. Perkins, bounding between her and the door of her room, toward which she was hastening; "you'll stay right here till this mystery is cleared up. For, if I understand Cap'n Steele aright, he can't find the property he left in this house, ner imagine what's become of it; an' you've been stuffing him with lies about Sam's running away with it. Am I right Cap'n?"

My father nodded, gazing with lowering brow upon the cowed and trembling form of the housekeeper.

"The Cap'n's property an' his savin's didn't walk away by themselves," continued Uncle Naboth, "and no one could' a' took 'em except Sam or this woman. Very good. They're both here, now, an' you're going to clear up the mystery and get your money back, Cap'n, before you takes your eye off'n either one. Just flop into that chair, Mrs. Ranck, an' if you try to wiggle away I'll call the police!"

The woman obeyed. A dull glaze had come over her eyes, and her features were white and set. In all her cunning plotting she had never imagined that I or my uncle would ever return to Batteraft to confound her. She believed that the knowledge that I was in her debt would prevent my coming back, in any event, and she fully expected me to be buffeted here and there about the world, with never a chance of my being again heard of in my old home.

What a mistake she had made! But it was all owing to this little fat man whom she had driven thoughtlessly from her door the day that I was sent away into exile. She had never heard of Naboth Perkins before; nor did she know, any more than I myself did at the time, of the partnership formerly existing between the two men, or even the fact of their relationship. She felt that she was caught in a trap, in some unexpected way, and the disaster stunned her.

Captain Steele filled and lighted his pipe before the silence of the little group was again broken. Then, turning to me, he asked:

"Why did you believe I was dead?"

"One of your sailors brought the news, sir, and told us of the wreck. He gave Mrs. Ranck your watch and ring, which he believed were taken from your dead body."

"It's a lie!" snapped the woman, desperately. "I never seen the watch and ring; but he said the Cap'n was dead, all right, an' that's why Sam run away with the property."

"Who was the sailor?" enquired my father, thoughtfully.

"Ned Britton, sir."

"Aye, an honest, worthy lad, who sailed with me for years. And he had the watch and ring?"

"Yes, sir. Ned was taken with a fever when he escaped from the wreck, and after he recovered they told him that several bodies had been washed ashore and buried by the villagers. On one of the bodies they found the watch and ring, so Ned naturally thought you had perished."

"When the ship broke up," said Captain Steele, slowly, "and I knew the end had come, I sent one of my lads to my cabin to get my trinkets while I attended to lowering the boats. I never saw him again. For my part, my leg was crushed by a falling mast, but I got entangled in the rigging and the mast floated me to a little island where a dozen fisher-folks lived. One was a bit of a doctor, and cut away my mangled leg and nursed me back to life. While I waited for a ship to touch the island I regained my strength and made myself a new leg out of cotton-wood. Then, one day, a schooner carried me to Plymouth, and the Captain, who was a kindly man, loaned me enough money to bring me to Batteraft where I thought I'd find my savings; enough to buy a new ship and start business again. But Mrs. Ranck met me with the news that my son had stripped the house of all my valuables and run away with a man that was known to be a pirate. My room was quite bare, I found, and Mrs. Ranck claimed she had hardly enough left of her savings to buy food with. So here I was, a cripple and condemned to poverty after a successful career; and it's no wonder my thoughts were bitter towards my son, whom I never would have believed could act so ungratefully. My only comfort was that Sam had believed me dead."

Uncle Naboth nodded approval.

"Quite proper, sir," he said, "an' all quite right and shipshape. Sam didn't take a penny's worth from this house; but I made him my partner, in your place, and we've had a successful voyage and come back rich as Croesuses. You'll live in clover, from this time on, Cap'n Steele, even if you never get back the property Mrs. Ranck has robbed you of. But why not make her give it up? She can't have squandered it on riotous living, by the looks of her."

Captain Steele turned to the housekeeper.

"What have you to say, Mrs. Ranck?" he asked.

194

"It's all a pack o' lies," she snarled, "but there's no call for you to believe me if you don't want to. One thing's certain, though. This is my house, an' the deed of it's in my name. You'll have to clear out o' here, all three of you, or I'll have the law on you an' put you out!"

Captain Steele arose calmly and seized the woman by her arms. In spite of her screams and struggles he carried her to his own little room and thrust her in, locking the door safely upon her.

"Now," said he, "let's explore the place and see what we can find. I've never been in Mrs. Ranck's room, for until today I had no suspicions of her. Come with me. If she's honest we shall find nothing, for she can't have disposed of the property."

"Right you are, sir," cried Uncle Naboth, springing up; and we all three at once proceeded to enter the room the housekeeper had for so many years reserved for her own use.

It was simply and plainly furnished, and a single glance served to convince us that it contained no evidence whatever of the missing property.

"Here's the treasure house, sir," he exclaimed triumphantly.

"Strange!" said my father, musingly. "There were nine cases and three chests, besides the great sea-chest that I found still in my room, although emptied of all its contents. Whatever could have become of them all?"

"Dad," I exclaimed, suddenly, "I remember there used to be a sort of cellar under this room, that could only be reached by a trap-door."

"True," replied my father; "I remember that, too. But where is the trap?"

Uncle Naboth was already making a careful inspection of the old rag carpet that covered the floor. In one corner the tacks seemed far apart and scanty. He seized the carpet and jerked it away from the fastenings, disclosing a small square trap with an iron ring in the center.

"Here's the treasure house, sir," he announced triumphantly.

"Get a candle, Sam," said my father, gravely.

When it was brought, all three of us descended the narrow stairs to the underground room, where the cases and chests were speedily found, all stored in orderly fashion against the walls. The contents of the great sea chest, which she had doubtless removed before admitting me to the Captain's room, had been placed in boxes which Mrs. Ranck had secured from the grocery store. In addition to Captain Steele's property, there was also a brass kettle almost full of gold and silver coins, which the miserly old woman had saved from the money my father had given her to clothe and care for me, as well as to defray the household expenses while the sailor was away upon his voyages.

Perhaps her own wages were added to this store, as

well; anyway, Captain Steele seemed to think so. For, after assuring himself that all his missing property was safe, he carried the kettle up to the living room and proceeded to liberate Mrs. Ranck. When, scowling but subdued, she crept from the little room, my father offered to give to her the entire contents of the kettle if she would freely transfer to him the deed to the house, and quit Batteraft for good and all.

"It's more than you deserve," said he, "but I don't want to go to the police in this matter unless you force me to. Take the money and go, and never let me see your face in Batteraft again."

Of course she accepted the generous proposition. After gathering her few clothes into a bundle, she took her treasure and left the house. The first train that left Batteraft carried her with it, and I have never seen her since.

I acknowledge that I watched her go with a lighter and happier heart than I had known for months.

"It was in this way that she once drove me from my old home, father," I said. "But it can't be such a bad world, after all. For, if the wicked sometimes appear to triumph, they are usually punished in the end, and now that Mrs. Ranck has passed out of our lives we ought to be very happy again."

"We will be, Sam!" returned my father, earnestly, as he affectionately pressed my hand.

"Hooray!" yelled Uncle Naboth.

CHAPTER XX.
STEELE, PERKINS AND STEELE.

Captain Steele was extremely grateful to Uncle Naboth for his care of me, and was delighted by the relation of our adventures on the golden island, as well as pardonably proud of the financial success we had attained.

A new firm was created under the title of "Steele, Perkins and Steele," and a new ship was soon found that seemed to have been especially constructed to meet our requirements. Captain Steele, declaring that his wooden leg would in no way interfere with his usefulness, decided to command the ship himself, and Ned Britton was made first mate. Uncle Naboth and I were appointed to look after all the finances and attend to the trading at the various ports, and Nux and Bryonia were brought from San Francisco and given posts on the new ship, to their great delight.

By the advice of his shrewder brother-in-law my father converted all his accumulated treasures into money, which was safely invested in Government bonds that were deposited in a Boston bank.

"Whatever happens now," observed Uncle Naboth, "nobody can't rob you again; and if our business ventures proves unsuccessful, and Sam and I go bankrupt, you've always got something to fall back on in your old age."

But success seemed to follow in the wake of the new

201

firm, and the "Cleopatra," as our ship is named, has made voyage after voyage with unvarying good fortune.

THE END.

www.ingramcontent.com/pod-product-compliance
Lightning Source LLC
Chambersburg PA
CBHW030543040726
47497CB00008B/2573